ISBN 978-1-331-25377-8
PIBN 10164785

1 MONTH OF
FREE
READING

at

www.ForgottenBooks.com

By purchasing this book you are eligible for one month membership to ForgottenBooks.com, giving you unlimited access to our entire collection of over 1,000,000 titles via our web site and mobile apps.

To claim your free month visit:

www.forgottenbooks.com/free164785

English
Français
Deutsche
Italiano
Español
Português

www.forgottenbooks.com

Mythology Photography **Fiction** Fishing Christianity **Art** Cooking Essays Buddhism Freemasonry Medicine **Biology** Music **Ancient Egypt** Evolution Carpentry Physics Dance Geology **Mathematics** Fitness Shakespeare **Folklore** Yoga Marketing **Confidence** Immortality Biographies Poetry **Psychology** Witchcraft Electronics Chemistry History **Law** Accounting **Philosophy** Anthropology Alchemy Drama Quantum Mechanics Atheism Sexual Health **Ancient History** **Entrepreneurship** Languages Sport Paleontology Needlework Islam **Metaphysics** Investment Archaeology Parenting Statistics Criminology **Motivational**

Cowboy Life on The Sidetrack

Being an Extremely Humorous and Sarcastic Story of the Trials and Tribulations Endured by a Party of Stockmen Making a Shipment from the West to the East.

By FRANK BENTON,
CHEYENNE, WYO.

ILLUSTRATED BY E. A. FILLEAU,
KANSAS CITY, MO.

DENVER, COLO.:
THE WESTERN STORIES SYNDICATE.

––––––––––

Press of
Hudson-Kimberly Publishing Company,
Kansas City, Mo.

DEDICATION.

For justice no shipper e'er asked in vain
From George H. Crosby or C. J. Lane.
We go to them, as to our dad,
When on their road our run is bad,
And when we think the freight too large
Ask them to rebate the overcharge.
No matter which road you give your freight,
To both these friends, this book I dedicate.

F. B.

The Author Waiting for the Train to Start.

CONTENTS.

PREFACE.

To the readers of this little booklet: I wish to say that while some things in the story seem overdrawn, yet I have endeavored to write it entirely from a cowboy standpoint.

To the sheepmen of the West: I want ·to say that I couldn't have written this story true to the cowboys' character without making a great many reflections on sheepmen, and I want to tender my apologies in advance for anything they may consider offensive, as some of my old-time and dearest friends in the West are among the large sheep owners. But I have been a cowboy and worked with the cowboys for thirty-two years, and have written the things set down here just as they came from the cowboys' lips on a stock train as we were waiting on sidetracks. The names of the cowboys used are the actual nicknames of cowpunchers whom I worked with on Wyoming ranges twenty years ago, and will be recognized by lots of old-timers.

9

The statement has been frequently made by newspapers that this volume was written as a roast on the Union Pacific railroad. I wish to correct that impression by saying that I selected that road for the groundwork of this story to give them a good advertisement free in requital for the many courtesies extended to me in times past by the officials of the road, for whom I have the warmest friendship.

THE AUTHOR.

Cowboy Life on The Sidetrack.

CHAPTER I.

THE START.

I met a man from Utah the other day by the name of Joe Smith, and he gave me quite an interesting history of his shipping some cattle to market over the great Overland route from Utah to South Omaha. I shall tell it in his own language. He said:

I don't want to misstate anything, and I don't want to exaggerate anything, but will tell you the plain facts.

When I and my neighbors, old Chuckwagon, Packsaddle Jack, Eatumup Jake and Dillbery Ike got into the ranch with a drive of cattle we found that three railroad live stock agents, two representatives of the union stockyards and five commission house drummers had been staying at the ranch for a week · waiting to get our shipment. Each one took each of us aside and gave us a dirty private as to what they would do for us. Every one of the commission house drummers said their house was second last month in number of cars of live stock in their market and they were looking for them to be first this month; said their salesmen always beat the other firms 10 cents a hundred on even splits, and their yardmen always got the best fill on the cattle. We went off by ourselves to talk it over and make up our minds which firm to ship to. Packsaddle Jack said it was remarkable that they all told the same story, said it was confusing as nary one of them had mentioned a point but what all the rest had coppered the same bet. Dillbery Ike gave it as his opinion that they were the bummest lot of liars he ever see. Old Chuckwagon and Eatumup Jake now compared notes and discovered that all the drummers were out of whiskey, but each drummer claimed the other dead beats had drank his up. Old Chuckwagon took a blue downhearted fit of melancholy on seeing they was all out of whiskey and wouldn't decide on any of them. Eatumup Jake just chewed a piece of dried rawhide and wouldn't talk. Packsaddle Jack and me finally decided to bill the cattle to ourselves till we got some further light on the subject.

Scott Davis Leaving to Order the Cars, and to Grease and Sand Them.

As the great Overland agent agreed that his road would run us all the way to market at the rate of forty miles an hour and the other live stock agents couldn't promise only thirty-five miles an hour, we gave the shipment to the Overland. The Overland agent went right into town to have the cars greased and sanded ready to start. We followed in with the cattle. It took us about seven days to drive the cattle in, and when we got there the cars were coming— but hadn't arrived. We waited around nine days, grazing the steers on sage brush in daytime and penning them nights till they got so thin we had about concluded to drive back and keep them for another year, when the cars came. It seemed the railroad had got them pretty near out to us once, but had run short of tonnage cars, so just had to haul them back and forth several times over one division to make up their tonnage for the trains. This was very annoying to the railroad men as well as ourselves, but they had their orders to not let any California fruit spoil on the road and to haul their tonnage, so just had to use these stock cars. It seems Harriman and Hill and J. P. Morgan and all the other boys who own the western railroads are very particular about every

2—

train hauling its full tonnage, and I heard there was places they had a lot of scrap iron close to the track, so if the train was short a ton or so they could load it on, haul it to some place where there was some freight to take the place of it, and then unload it for trains going the other way that were short on tonnage.

Finally we got the cattle loaded and our contract signed. Got a basket of grub, as we were informed there would be no time to get meals on the road. It is to this basket of grub that we all owe our lives to-day, so I will give a partial description of the contents. First, we had four dozen bottles of beer; next, eight quarts of old rye whiskey; next, two corkscrews, a hard boiled egg, a sandwich without any meat in it and a bottle of mustard, as Dillbery Ike said he always wanted mustard. Eatumup Jake was for getting a can of tomatoes, but old Chuckwagon said he never had been empty of canned tomatoes in twenty years and wanted one chance to get them out his system.

Well, we got on the way-car, were hitched on to the cattle train and off at last for the first sidetrack, which was a quarter of a mile from the stockyards.

The conductor said we would start right away soon as he got his orders, so Chuckwagon proposed we open the lunch, which meeting with direct approval from the entire party, we proceeded to consume a large section of it, and then went to sleep. When we woke up the sun was sinking in the east, at least I maintained it was east, but Packsaddle Jack said it was in the north. Anyway we argued till it sunk, and never did agree. But we found we were on the same old sidetrack, and as our lunch was about gone we made up a jackpot and sent Dillbery Ike after more lunch. Packsaddle Jack went up and interviewed the agent in the meantime, as he was the only one left in the party who was on speaking terms with that functionary, and found out they were holding us there for the arrival of eight cars of sheep that was expected to come by trail from Idaho. These sheep belong to Rambolet Bill and old Cottswool Canvasback, and these two gentlemen had seen a cloud of dust ten miles away about noon and insisted on having the train held, as they were sure the sheep were coming, which finally proved to be correct. So when they got them loaded, about 11 o'clock that night, we quit quarrelling with the agent, stopped making threats against the railroad superintendent, got Dillbery Ike to put on his coat (he had kept if off all evening to whip the railroad agent who was to blame undoubtedly for all this delay), and finally started, with rising spirits. But as we got up to the depot where the conductor was waiting with his final papers, the head brakeman reported a cow was down up near the engine, and we all walked up there and found that one of Dillbery Ike's critters had become so weak and emaciated that it had succumbed right in the start. We prodded her, and hollered and yelled, and Chuckwagon twisted her tail clear off before we discovered she was stiff and cold in death and consequently couldn't respond to our suggestions. Dillbery asked the advice of a hobo (who was giving us pointers how to get her up before we discovered her dead condition) about suing the railroad company for her. The hobo agreed to act as witness and swear to anything after Dillbery gave him a nip out of his bottle; and after we found out what a good fellow the hobo was, how much he knew about shipping cattle and that he wanted to go east, we concluded to put his name on the contract and make him one of the party. We asked his name and he said 'twas most always John Doe, but we nicknamed him Jackdo for short.

We all went back to the way-car and started up to the switch and back on to a sidetrack, as No. 1 was expected to arrive pretty soon, as she was four hours late, and was liable to come any time after she got four hours late.

After taking some lunch we lay down on the seats and went to sleep, Jackdo, Rambolet Bill and Cotts-wool Canvasback on one side of the car, and Dillbery Ike, Chuckwagon, Packsaddle Jack, Eatumup Jake and myself on the other side. It was rather crowded on our side of the car, but none of us liked the perfume that Jackdo and the two sheepmen used. About the time we got to sleep the brakeman came in, woke us all up so he could get into the coal and kindling which is under the seat in a way-car. It was warm weather, but the train crews always build roaring fires in hot weather on stock trains, and he was only following the usual custom. We got our places again and dropped off to sleep. The conductor came in, woke us all up to punch our contracts. We went to sleep again; the conductor came around, roused us all up to know where we wanted our stock fed. Jackdo now gave us a great deal of advice about where to feed and how much, but Dillbery said the cattle had got used to going without feed so long that it wasn't worth while to waste time feeding them now. Jackdo said all the stockmen fed plenty of hay to their stock all the way to Omaha, but never let them have any water till they got there, as they would get a big fill that way. We finally went to sleep again. The conductor and brakeman took turns jumping down out of their high airy cab on top of the car (where they keep a window open) to build up the fire and see that all the doors and windows below were tightly closed so the stockmen couldn't get no air, but hot air. However, we had been getting hot air from the railroad live stock agents and commission house drummers for some time and slept on till old Chuckwagon begun to snore and woke us up again. It seemed he was having a fearful nightmare, and we had all we could do to keep him from jumping off the train till we got him fairly awake. But after we had each given him a drink from our private bottles he gave several long, shuddering, shivering sighs and told us his dream.

CHAPTER II.

CHUCKWAGON'S DREAM.

He said he dreamed he was in a deep narrow canyon, and it seemed to be a very hot day, and he thought he walked in the broiling hot sun for miles and miles, his mouth and throat parched with thirst and his eyes almost bursting from their sockets with the heat, when all at once he heard the low mutterings of thunder and he knew there was a storm approaching. The thunder kept growing louder and louder, and he looked around for some shelter and discovered a narrow crevice in the rocks, and just as the storm broke he entered this crevice. He hadn't no more than got inside when he saw a wild animal approaching the same place of refuge. It was bigger than any two grizzly bears he ever saw in his life, but was black with white stripes down its back, had a large bushy tail, and he knew he was up against the biggest skunk the world had ever known, and trembling with horror he crept farther and farther back into the

21

crevice till he was stopped by a stream of red molten fire that seemed to be flowing across his path in the mountain. He was about to retreat, but as he turned to retrace his steps the immense Jumbo skunk was coming in the crevice backwards with its enormous tail reared over its back, and while the crevice seemed only just large enough for him, yet this great animal had a way of flattening himself out that, while he was a great deal taller than before, yet did he keep forcing himself gradually back towards poor Chuck. Chuck-wagon said he knew that if the skunk was disturbed he would discharge that terrible effluvia that is known the world over, yet the heat from the molten stream of fire was so great that it burned his face and he was obliged to keep it turned towards the skunk. Finally the animal had backed so far that the top of Chuck-wagon's head was just under the root of the skunk's tail. Then something commenced to annoy the animal in front, and it started to back a little farther. It was then he gave that despairing, blood-curdling, soul-freezing yell that woke us up, and he said he could still smell that awful effluvia even now that he was awake; but we told him it was just the heat of the car and the perfume that Jackdo and the two sheepmen had.

We now discovered that the train was in motion. We were in doubt a long time, but after marking fence posts, setting up a line of sticks and testing it by all the known devices, we became convinced that it was really a fact, and when there was no longer any doubt left in our minds we fell on each other's necks and sobbed for joy. We tapped four fresh bottles in succession to celebrate the event and shook one another's hands repeatedly. But, alas! in the midst of our rejoicing we came to a sidetrack.

It seems to be one of the rules of railroading to never pass a sidetrack with a stock train till they find out whether that particular train will fit that sidetrack. This sidetrack was 2,125 feet and 223 inches long and our train just fit it like it had been made a purpose. If our train had been three feet longer it would have been too long for this sidetrack, and we had a long heated argument whether the train had been made for this sidetrack or the sidetrack designed for this special train; but, anyway, I never saw a better fit, and it shows what mechanical heads railroad men have got. We became attached to this sidetrack, and for a long time had the sole use of it. We held it against all comers, trains of empty cars going west, gravel cars and even handcars, but finally had to leave it, and it was with feelings of sadness and regret that we at last had to bid it good-bye. Although we had many sidetracks afterwards, yet as this one was the first we had entirely to ourselves we hated to give it up and our eyelashes were wet with unshed tears as we blew the last kisses from our finger tips when it slowly faded from our sight around a narrow bend in the roadbed. How long it remained true to us we never knew, probably not long, as it was a lonely spot and undoubtedly was occupied by another stock train as soon as we were out of sight.

While at this sidetrack we took a stroll over the hills one day and found a sage hen's nest with the old hen setting. Dillbery Ike slipped up, grasped her by the tail and in her struggle to free herself she lost all her tail feathers and got away. Dillbery tied a string around the tail feathers and took them along. This, as it turned out afterwards, was very fortunate, as we were able by the feathers to settle a dispute that might have led to serious consequences, which happened in this way: Some time after the sage hen episode, while we were waiting on a sidetrack one day for a gravel train going west, and having had nothing to eat for a long time but mustard on ice, we had become very much discouraged and had even tried to buy Cottswool Canvasback's coat to make soup of, when Jackdo discovered a flock of half-grown young sage chickens feeding along past the train, and immediately we were all out, filled our hats with rocks and commenced to knock them over. We managed to kill the most of them along with the old mother bird, and made the startling discovery that she had lost her tail feathers. We showed her to the division superintendent, who came along in his private car just then and stopped to explain some of the delays on our run, and told him the story of Dillbery pulling out her tail when she was setting. The superintendent argued it couldn't be the same hen, but when Dillbery got the bunch of tail feathers they just fitted in the holes in the poor old bird's rump and that settled the dispute.

There was another little incident occurred afterwards that shows the world isn't so large after all. One day while we were waiting on a sidetrack a mud turtle came strolling by, and as Jackdo had suggested turtle soup for old Chuckwagon, who, by the way, had been feeling bad ever since the night he had the skunk dream, not being able to keep anything on his stomach, we captured the turtle and on examining a peculiar mark on the back of its shell discovered it was Dillbery Ike's brand that he had playfully burnt into the animal the day before we left the ranch with the cattle.

Rambolet Bill, Cottswool Canvasback and Jackdo Watching the Sheep Graze.

CHAPTER III.

GRAZING THE SHEEP.

It's not generally known that when sheep get extremely hungry they eat the wool off one another, but nevertheless this is a fact, and Cottswool Canvasback and Rambolet Bill's sheep had long ere this devoured all the wool off each other's backs, but we had had a couple good warm showers of rain and the wool had started up again and was high enough for pretty fair grazing, so the two sheepmen were middlin' easy, as they had a receipt for cooking jackrabbits so they wouldn't shrink in the cooking. They claimed that Manager Gleason of the Warren Live Stock Company had invented this receipt. However, lambing season had come on and Cottswool and Rambolet were kept pretty busy as double deck cars was very cramped quarters to lamb in. Rambolet wanted to unload the sheep, and when they got through lambing to drive them to Laramie City and catch the train again, but Cottswool Canvasback said they would have to pay the same tariff for the cars and insisted on the railroad company earning their money.

Jackdo Sings "Home, Sweet Home."

I remember a pathetic little incident that occurred about this time. When we were waiting on a sidetrack one evening I suggested to Jackdo that he sing us a song to while away the time, and he started in singing "Home, Sweet Home," in a choked-by-cinders sort of voice, and he hadn't been singing long before I discovered old Chuckwagon and Dillbery Ike lying face downward on the seats sobbing like their hearts would break. Chuck and Dillbery didn't have much of a home, as they batched in little dobe shacks away out on the edge of the plains; but that old song, even if sung by a hoot owl, would make a stockman weep when he is on a stock train and has got about half-way to market. However, it didn't seem to affect Eatumup Jake much, and yet Jake had married a big, buxom, red-headed Mormon girl about six weeks before we started to ship. While Jake looked like he was in delicate health when we left home, yet he had grown strong and hearty on the trip in spite of the privations and sufferings we had to go through, and was pretty near always whistling in a lively way "The Girl I Left Behind Me."

We now arrived at a town. It was about two o'clock in the morning and the conductor roused us up to tell us we would have to change way-cars, as they didn't go any farther. We asked him which way to go when we got off, and he said go anyway we wanted to. We asked him where our car was that we would go out on, and he said, "Damfino." So we started out to hunt it. This was a division station, there were hundreds of cars in every direction and they had put us off a mile from the depot. We begged piteously from everyone we met to tell us where the way-car was that went out on the stock train. We carried our luggage back and forth, fell over switch frogs in the darkness and skinned our shins, fell over one another trying to keep out the way of switch engines, ran ourselves out of breath after brakemen, conductors, engineers and car oilers, but everyone of them gave us the same stereotyped answer, "Damfino." At last we started out to hunt up the stock again, but just as we found it they started to switching. However, we climbed on the sides of the cars and hung on, all but poor old Chuckwagon, who had been sorter under the weather and wasn't quite quick enough. But he chased manfully after us till

3—

we came to a switch, when we dashed past him going the other way. We hollered to him to follow the train, which he did, but only to find us going the other way again. And thus we kept on. How long this would have lasted I don't know, for old Chuck was game to the death and had throwed away his coat, vest, hat and boots and was bound to catch them stock cars, and the switchman and engineer was bound he shouldn't. But finally the engine had to stop for coal and water, and they shoved us in on a sidetrack, went off to bed and left us there till 10 o'clock the next day. But I never shall forget the anguish and horror we endured for fear we wouldn't find that way-car and they would pull the stock out and leave us there. Packsaddle Jack gave its as his opinion that the railroad people had plotted to do that, but we frustrated their designs by getting on the stock cars and staying with them. We all believed Packsaddle Jack was right, but since that time I've talked with a good many cattlemen and found out that's the way they treat everybody.

CHAPTER IV.

LETTERS FROM HOME BROUGHT BY IMMIGRANTS.

We arrived at Rawlins, Wyoming, one bright sunny morning and planned to get a square meal there and kinder clean up and take a shave. But this was a sheep town and full of sheepmen and the odor of sheep was so strong we just stopped long enough to fill our bottles and then sauntered on ahead of our train, expecting to get on when it overtook us. Well, we sauntered and sauntered, looking back from every hill, but no train, and finally when we were tired from walking in the heat and dust we found a shade tree, and, laying down, went to sleep. How long we slept I don't know, but when we awoke it was night. In the darkness we had hard work finding our way back to the railroad track, and for a while were undecided which way to go, but finally took the wrong direction, and after plodding along in the dark for several miles we came on top a high hill and saw the lights of the town below us that we left that morning. We now held a council as to who should go down to town to get our bottles filled. Jackdo offered to go, but we had already discovered we couldn't trust him on that kind of errand, as the bottles would be just as empty when he got back as when he started, so finally we sent Eatumup Jake and told him to inquire if our train was still there or had gone sneaking by us when we were asleep. Jake returned about midnight with the refreshments and the information that the train was on ahead. So we started after it, exchanging ideas along the route as to how far we would have to walk before we came to a sidetrack, as we didn't doubt for a moment we would find the stock on the first siding it could get in on. This was one of the pleasantest nights we had on our whole trip, with good fresh air (we made the sheepmen and Jackdo walk about three miles ahead of us and the wind was blowing in their direction) and nothing to worry us. We talked of home and speculated as to how many calves the boys at home had branded for us on their annual roundups since we left.

Finally Chuckwagon stopped and sniffed a time or two and said he was satisfied the sheepmen and Jackdo must have found the train. After we walked a mile further we came to the sheepmen and Jackdo setting down at a sidetrack, but the stock train was not there. We were much puzzled at this, but after a great deal of argument Eatumup Jake, who had studied Arithmetic some, proposed to measure the sidetrack. He suggested as the only possible solution to the train not being there that probably the track was too short for the train. The trouble now was to get some proper thing to measure with. Finally we took Eatumup Jake's pants which he had removed for the purpose, they being thirty-four inches inseam. By taking the end of each leg they measured sixty-eight inches, or five feet eight inches, to a measurement. Every time we made a measurement Dillbery put a pebble in his pocket for feet and Chuckwagon put one in his for inches. When we got through we made a light out of some sticks and counted the pebbles. Dillbery had 292 and Chuckwagon 287. They both insisted they had made no mistake, so we had to measure it all over again. There had come up a little flurry of snow in the meantime, which happens frequently at that altitude, and Eatumup Jake wanted them to divide the difference between 287 and 292, but as one had inches and the other feet, Eatumup Jake couldn't make the

proper division in his head and we had nothing to figure with. So we measured again and counted and
found they each had 287. As this would only equal
forty-one stock cars, and as there was forty-three cars
of stock, five cars of California fruit, three cars mer-
chandise, nine tonnage cars and the way-car, we knew
our train couldn't possibly get in on this sidetrack. So
Jake put on his pants and we started on again, perfectly satisfied now that we had solved what seemed
at first a great mystery.

After walking several miles it became daylight
and we discovered a man and woman with a mule team
and wagon, going the same way we were. As they
didn't seem to have much of a load and asked us to
ride we concluded to ride. However, as we couldn't
all ride in the wagon at once and as the wagon road
wasn't always in sight of the track, we had Jackdo
and the two sheepmen walk along the track, and if
they found the train they were to holler and wave
something to us so we would know.

Eatumup Jake had been kinder grumpy ever since
he had to stand the snowstorm without any pants on
while we done the measuring, but now he was to hear
some good news which brought such overwhelming

joy to him as, indeed, it did to all of us, as our joys and sorrows were one on this trip. It will be remembered that Eatumup Jake had married a buxom Mormon girl about six weeks before we started with the cattle, and now it turned out that these people, who were on their way from the Two Wallys to Arkansas, had come by Jake's place in Utah and Jake's wife had not only sent a letter by this couple to him, but the letter contained the news that he was the father of twin boys. Jake's pride and joy knew no bounds, and for a time he talked about going back and taking a look at the twins and then catching up to us again. But we argued this would bring bad luck, and anyway there were immigrants on the way from Oregon to Arkansas all the time, and Jake's wife said all our folks in Utah had agreed to send us letters every time anyone came by with a team going east.

We now came in sight of our stock train as it was slowly climbing a grade, but we were loath to give up our new-found friends, the immigrants, and 't wasn't till they had drove several miles ahead of the stock train that we finally bid them a reluctant good-bye . and sauntered on back to meet the special. This is the first time I've used the word special, but all stock trains are known as specials because they make special time with them.

After we got on the train and had taken the prod pole, and drove the sheepmen and Jackdo out and made them ride on top, we emptied a bottle or so and Eatumup Jake got very hilarious and sang "The Little Black Bull Came Running Down the Mountain," while we all joined in the chorus. And finally when old Chuckwagon, Packsaddle Jack and Dillbery Ike had gone to sleep on the floor of the car, Eatumup Jake got me by the button hole and told me the story of his life in the following words. He talked in a thick, slushy, slobbery voice, somethingg like the mud and water squirts through the holes in your overshoes on a sloppy day, but this was on account of a great deal of whiskey and the fact that he had taken a slight cold the night before standing in the snowstorm while we used his pants to measure the sidetrack.

CHAPTER V.

EATUMUP JAKE'S LIFE STORY.

He said his father was a poor Methodist preacher in a little country place in western Kansas where he was born. Said they lived there many years because they was so durn poor they couldn't get away. His father's salary was paid promptly every month in contributions and consisted of one sack of cornmeal, one sack of potatoes, two gallons sorghum molasses, four old crowing hens, seven jack rabbits, one quart choke cherry jelly and one load of dried buffalo chips for fuel. He said his father was one of the most patient beggars he ever saw, that he took up collections at all times and on all occasions, morning, noon and night —week days and Sundays he passed the hat. He had seventeen different kinds of foreign missions to beg for. He had twenty-one different kinds of home missions to beg for, and while it was the poorest community he ever saw, most people too poor to have any tea or coffee, or overshoes for winter or shoes in summer, yet his father begged so persistently that he got worlds of flannels for the heathens in Africa, any amount of bibles for the starving children in New York City and all kinds of religious literature for the reconcentrados in India.

Finally his mother died of nothing on the stomach, his father and a woman missionary went to Chicago, his nine brothers and sisters was bound out and adopted by different people, and he, the oldest child, was taken in charge by a professional bone picker, and although he was only 10 years old at the time, yet he picked up bones on Kansas prairies summer and winter for two years till a bunch of cowpunchers came along and took him away from the bone picker. He said he never had anything much to eat till he got into this cow camp, and just eat roast veal, baking powder biscuits, plum duff and California canned goods till all the cowboys stopped eating to look at him, and one of them asked his name, and when he said Jacob, they immediately nicknamed him Eatumup Jake.

He said he never had seen any of his folks since all this happened, but one night he had a dream, just as plain as day. He thought he was in a big city and a one-legged man with blue glasses was following him, and when he stopped the man said: "Jacob, I'm your father," and he asked him how he lost his leg, what he was wearing blue glasses for (a placard saying he was blind), and why he held out a tincup, and his father said: "I aint lost any leg, it's tied up inside my pants leg, and I'm wearing glasses so people can't see my eyes." And he. said his father told him that his training as a Methodist preacher had peculiarly fitted him for a professional beggar.

When Eatumup Jake finished telling his story he fell to weeping and wept very bitterly for a long time, and when I tried to comfort him by telling him a man wasn't to blame for what his folks done, he said no, but cowmen were to blame when they fell so durn low as to spend the best part of their lives on a special stock train associating with a hobo and two sheepmen.

CHAPTER VI.

THE SCHOOLMARM'S SADDLE HORSE.

One day while waiting on a sidetrack old Chuck-wagon got to telling about the new schoolmarm in their neighborhood. He said he reckoned she was as high educated as anybody ever got. He said she didn't sabe cowpuncher talk much, but she used some mighty high-sounding words. Why, he said, she called a watergap a wateryawn; a shindig, a dawnce; Injuns, Naborigines; cowboys, cow servants, and Bill Allen's hired girl, where she boards, a domestic. The first night she came to Bill Allen's she heard them a talking about cowpunchers, and she asked old Bill if he wouldn't show her a real live cowpuncher; said there weren't any cowpunchers in Boston, where she came from, and old Bill said he'd have one over from the nearest cow ranch next day.

So next morning he comes over to my ranch and tells me to rig out in fur shaps, put on my buckskin shirt and big Mexican hat with tassels on it, with red silk handkerchief around my neck, and he would take

42

George H. Crosby, General Freight Agent B. & M.

me over and introduce me to the new schoolmarm.
So I rigged all up proper, and when we got over to
Bill Allen's place, old Bill told his wife to go to the
schoolmarm's room and tell her he had a genuine cowpuncher out there and for her to come out and see
him. She told Mrs. Allen she was busy just then, but
tell Mr. Allen to take the cowpuncher to the barn and
give him some hay and she would be out directly.

Now, he'd been wondering ever since, old Chuck
said, what on earth she reckoned a cowpuncher was.
Still she was mighty green about some things, 'cause
when they had a little party at old Bill Allen's all the
girls got to telling about the breed of their saddle
hosses, and some said their hoss was a Hamiltonian,
and some said their hoss was thoroughbred, and some
was Blackhawk Morgan. The schoolmarm said she
had a gentleman friend in Boston who had a very
fine saddle hoss of the stallion breed, and when the
boys giggled and the gals began to look red, she says
as innocent as a lamb. "There is such a breed of
hosses, ain't they?" "Of course," she says, "I know
it's a rare breed and perhaps you folks out here never
saw any of that breed." She says, "They are great
hosses to whinney. Why, my friend's hoss kept

whinneying all the time." When she got to describ-
ing that hoss's habits, course all us boys begun to
back up and git out the room. I reckon she was
from an Irish family, 'cause she insisted Mrs. Flana-
gan was right when she called the station a daypo.

But I reckon she could just knock the hind
sights off anybody when it came to singing. I never
did know just whether it was a song or not she sung,
'cause none of us could understand it. She said it
was Italian, and of course there wasn't any of us un-
derstood any Dago talk. But she would just commence away down in a kind of low growl, like a
sleeping foxhound when he is dreaming of a bear
fight, and keep growling a little louder and little
louder, and directly begin to give some short barks,
and then it would sound like a herd of wild cattle
bawling round a dead carcass; then like a lot of hungry coyotes howling of a clear frosty night, and
finally wind up like hundreds of wild geese flying high
and going south for winter. She said her voice had
been cultivated and I reckon it had. You could tell
it had been laid off in mighty even rows, the weeds
all pulled out and the dirt throwed up close to the
hills. But somehow I'd a heap rather hear a little

blue-eyed girl I know up in the mountains in Idaho sing "The Suwanee River," and "Coming Through the Rye," 'cause I can understand that. But I guess them Boston girls are all right at home. I reckon they are used to them there.

CHAPTER VII.

SELLING CATTLE ON THE RANGE.

Then old Packsaddle Jack got to telling about
Senator Dorsey, of Star Route fame, selling a little
herd of cattle he had in northern New Mexico. He
said the Senator had got hold of some eye-glass
Englishmen, and representing to them that he had a
large herd of cattle in northern New Mexico, finally
made a sale at $25 a head all round for the cattle.
The Englishmen, however, insisted on counting the
herd and wouldn't take the Senator's books for them.
Dorsey finally agreed to this, but said the cattle
would have to be gathered first. The Senator then
went to his foreman, Jack Hill, and asked Jack if he
knew of a place where they could drive the cattle
around a hill where they wouldn't have to travel too
far getting around and have a good place to count
them on one side. Jack selected a little round mountain with a canyon on one side of it, where he sta-
tioned the Englishmen and their bookkeepers and

48

Senator Dorsey. The Senator had about 1,000 cattle, and Jack and the cowboys separated them into two bunches out in the hills, a couple of miles from the party of Englishmen and out of sight. Keeping the two herds about a mile apart, they now drove the first herd into the canyon, which ran around the edge of the bluff, and on the bank of the canyon sat the Senator with the Englishmen, and they counted the cattle as the herd strung along by them. The herd was hardly out of sight before the second bunch came stringing along. Two or three cowboys, though, had met the first herd, and, getting behind them, galloped them around back of the mountain and had them coming down the canyon past the Englishmen again, and they were counted the second time. And they were hardly out of sight before the second division was around the mountain and coming along to be tallied some more. And thus the good work went on all day long, the Senator and the Englishmen only having a few minutes to snatch a bite to eat and tap fresh bottles.

The foreman told the English party at noon that they was holding an enormous herd back in the hills yet from which they were cutting off these small bunches of 500 and bringing them along to be tallied. But along about 3 o'clock in the afternoon the cattle began to get thirsty and footsore. Every critter had traveled thirty miles that day, and lots of them began to drop out and lay down. In one of the herds was an old yellow steer. He was bobtailed, lophorned and had a game leg, and for the fifteenth time he limped by the crowd that was counting. Milord screwed his eyeglass a little tighter into his eye, and says, "There is more bloody, blarsted, lophorned, bobtailed, yellow, crippled brutes than anything else, don't you know." Milord's dogrobber speaks up, and says, "But, me lord, there's no 'hanimal like 'im hin the hither 'erd."

The Senator overheard this interesting conversation, and taking the foreman aside, told him when they got that herd on the other side of the mountain again to cut out that old yellow reprobate, and not let him come by again. So Jack cut him out and run him off aways in the mountains. But old yellow had got trained to going around that mountain, and the herd wasn't any more than tallied again till here come old Buck, as the cowboys called him, limping along behind down the canyon, the Englishmen staring at him with open mouths, and Senator Dorsey looking at old Jack Hill in a reproachful, grieved kind of way. The cowboys ran old Buck off still-farther next time, but half an hour afterwards he appeared over a little rise and slowly limped by again.

The Senator now announced that there was only one herd more to count and signaled to Jack to ride around and stop the cowboys from bringing the bunches around any more, which they done. But as the party broke up and started for the ranch, old Buck came by again, looking like he was in a trance, and painfully limped down the canyon. That night the cowboys said the Senator was groaning in his sleep in a frightful way, and when one of them woke him up and asked if he was sick, he told them, while big drops of cold sweat was dropping off his face, that he'd had a terrible nightmare. He thought he was yoked up with a yellow, bobtailed, lophorned, lame steer and was being dragged by the animal through a canyon and around a mountain day after day in a hot, broiling sun, while crowds of witless Englishmen and jibbering cowboys were looking on. He insisted on saddling up and going back through the moonlight to the mountain and see if old Buck was still there. When they arrived, after waiting awhile, they heard something coming down the canyon, and in the bright moonlight they could see old Buck painfully limping along, stopping now and then to rest.

A cowboy reported finding old Buck dead on his well-worn trail a week afterwards. But no one ever rides that way moonlight nights now, as so many cowboys have a tradition that old Buck's ghost still limps down the canyon moonlight nights.

Counting "Old Buck."

OLD BUCK'S GHOST.

———

Down in New Mexico, where the plains are brown and sere,
There is a ghostly story of a yellow spectral steer.
His spirit wanders always when the moon is shining bright;
One horn is lopping downwards, the other sticks upright.

On three legs he comes limping, as the fourth is sore and lame;
His left eye is quite sightless, but still this steer is game.
Many times he was bought and counted by a dude with a mon-
    ocle in his eye;
The steer kept limping round a mountain to be counted by that
    guy.

When footsore, weary, gasping, he laid him down at last,
His good eye quit its winking; counting was a matter of the
    past;
But his spirit keeps a tramping 'round that mountain trail,
And that's the cause, says Packsaddle, that I have told this
    tale.

CHAPTER VIII.

True Snake Stories.

Then we all got to telling true snake stories. Eatumup Jake said down on the Republican River in western Kansas the rattle-snakes were awful thick when the country was first settled. He said they had their dens in the Chalk Bluffs along the Republican and Solomon rivers; said these bluffs were full of them. It was nothing for the first settlers in that country to get together of a Sunday afternoon in the fall of the year and kill 15,000 rattle-snakes at one bluff as they lay on the shelves of rock that projected out from its face. He said the snake dens were two or three miles apart, all the way along the river for a hundred miles, and when somebody would start in to killing them at one place, why all the snakes at that den would start in to rattling. Then the snakes at the dens on each side of where they was killing them would wake up and hear their neighbors' rattle, and then they'd get mad and begin to rattle and that would wake up

56

the snake dens beyond them and start them to rattling. And in an hour's time all the snakes for a
hundred miles along that country would be rattling.
When these two hundred million snakes all got to
rattling at once you could hear them one hundred
miles away and all the settlers in eastern Kansas
would go into their cyclone cellars. But after the
Populists got so thick in Kansas, if they did hear the
snakes get to rattling, they just thought five or six
Populists got together and was talking politics.

Then Packsaddle Jack told about a bull-snake
family he used to know in southern Kansas. He
said the whole family had yellow bodies beautifully
marked below the waist, but from their waist up, in-
cluding their necks and heads, was a shiny coal black.
The old man bull-snake would beller just like a bull
when he was stirred up. The old lady bull-snake had
sort of an alto voice and the younger master and
misses bull-snakes went from soprano and tenor down
to a hiss. He said this family of bull-snakes were
very proud of their clothes, as there weren't any other
bull-snakes dressed like them, all the other bull-
snakes being just a plain yellow. And old Mrs. Bull-
snake used to talk about her ancestors on her fa-

ther's side, and she called the scrubby willow under which they had their den the family tree, and talked about the family tree half her time. She never allowed her daughters to associate with any of the common young bull-snakes, but kept them coiled up around home under the family tree till they got very delicate, being in the shade all the time. All the snakes in the country looked up to this family of half-black bull-snakes and they were known by the name of Half-Blacks. All the old female bull-snakes in the country around there, if they had just a distant speaking acquaintance with Mrs. Half-Black, always spoke of her as "my dear intimate friend Mrs. Half-Black." Old Papa Half-Black set around all swelled up with unwary toads he'd swallowed when they came under the family tree for shade, and while he didn't say much about his ancestry and family tree, yet he was mighty proud and dignified. Sometimes he would slip off from his illustrious family, and going over the hill where there was a little sand blow-out and something to drink, he'd meet some of the Miss Common Bull-snakes, and then he would unbend a good deal from his dignity and treat them with great familiarity, and after having a few drinks call them his sweethearts and get them to sing "The Good Old Summer Time," and he would join in the chorus with his heavy bass voice, and they would all be very gay. Of course, he never told old Mrs. Half-Black about these meetings, cause she wouldn't understand them.

But with all their glory this aristocratic family of half-black bull-snakes came to an untimely end. One day there came along a couple of mangy Kansas hogs and rooted the whole family out and eat them up as fast as they came to them; rooted up the family tree also.

We all cheered Packsaddle Jack's bull-snake story.

We now all got to telling stories about fellows we knowed who had died from mad skunk bites, said skunks creeping up on them in the night when they were sleeping outdoors. When we got to the end of our mad skunk stories we turned our attention to tales of friends of ours who had died from rattle-snake bites. It seemed each of us had dozens of dead friends who had met their doom by crawling into a roundup bed at night without shaking the blankets only to find a couple of rattle-snakes coiled up inside. The more we told the stories the more snake-bite antidote we imbibed, till we got so full of the antidote it's safe to say that it would have been sure death for any poisonous reptile to have bitten any man in the crowd. Some of us wept a good deal over the memory of our dead friends and other things, and all together this was about the most enjoyable half day of our journey.

CHAPTER IX.

Chuckwagon's Death.

I now come to a point in my story that is fraught with such grief and sorrow that I would gladly pass over if I could, but my story wouldn't be complete without this sad chapter.

We were slowly climbing Sherman Hill, some of us pushing on the train, some using pinch bars—as we always did where there was a hard pull—when all of a sudden the engine broke down and the train started slowly back down the hill. While the train didn't go very fast on account that the wheels hadn't been greased since we started, as the company was economizing on oil, and the train stopped when it got to the bottom of the hill, yet it was so discouraging and heart-sickening to poor old Chuckwagon that he died almost immediately after this took place.

He had been gradually growing weaker lately, not being able to keep anything on his stomach except a little Limburger cheese since the night he had the skunk dream. He always imagined this dream to be a warning, and had low sinking spells at times, specially when the two sheepmen and Jackdo were all three in the car in at once, and at such times we were obliged to take a prod pole and drive Jackdo and the two sheepmen out the car and make them ride on top till Chuck revived. We made some smelling salts out of asafœtida and Limburger cheese for him to use when he had these fainting spells, as he frequently did when the car got warm and Jackdo and the sheepmen were there. We also found the decomposed body of a dog lying beside the track one day, and gathering it up in a gunnysack would hang it round Chuck's neck at night when the sheepmen and Jackdo had to ride inside, and in that way he would get a little sleep. But if he happened to be out of reach of any of these remedies when one of the sheepmen come near him he immediately began to strike at the end of his nose and mutter something about glue factories.

Poor old Chuckwagon! In my mind I can still see his ruggged, tear-stained face as he would piteously hold out his hands for his sack of decomposed dog when one of the sheepmen or Jackdo came in the way-car.

All I know of Chuckwagon's life before he come West was what he told me on this trip. He said as a boy he had worked cleaning sewers in Chicago and after that was watchman for glue factories till he come West, but with all this training had never got hardened enough to stand the smell of Jackdo, Cottswool Canvasback and Rambolet Bill in a way-car.

He died like a hero. When we see he was going, Packsaddle Jack took a prod pole and drove Jackdo and the sheepmen down the track aways so Chuck could breathe some purer air. Then we gave him a whiff of decomposed dog, propped him up against an old railroad tie and took his post-mortem statement in writing as to cause of his death. We let some cattlemen who had formed themselves into a committee for the public safety up in the New Fork country, in Wyoming, have his statement. We now went to the nearest town, got the best coffin we could and after selecting a place right under a big cliff, we buried old Chuck and piled up a lot of rock at the grave so we could come back and get him and give him a good decent burial on his own ranch. We didn't have much funeral services, but Dillbery Ike made a talk which just filled all our ideas exactly, and here is what he said:

DILLBERY IKE'S TRIBUTE TO CHUCKWAGON.

Chuck was a good man. While he never joined church and drunk a heap of whiskey, bucked faro and monte, cussed mighty hard at times, yet he always paid his debts. Never killed other people's beef and didn't take mavericks till they was plum weaned from the cows. He believed mighty strong in ghosts and God Almighty; believed in angels, 'cause he loved a little, blonde, blue-eyed girl away up in the mountains in Idaho. He had a strong belief in heaven, but a heap stronger one in hell, 'cause he said there must be some place to keep the sheepmen by themselves in the other world. He never had a father or mother and no bringing up, but lived a better life 'cording to what he knowed than some people who knowed more. He always gave his big-jawed cattle to Injuns to eat, place of hauling the meat to town and peddling it out to white folks. He'd been known to even cut stove wood for married men when their wives were off visiting, and once he gave all the tobacco and cigarette papers he had to a sick Digger Injun and went without for a week himself. He always let the tenderfoot visitor at the ranch fish all the strips of bacon out the beans and pretended to be looking the other way, and when old Widow Mulligan, who ran a little milk ranch, died of fever and left four little red-headed kids he took them all home and took care of them, told them bear stories till they all went to sleep nights in his bed, washed them, fed them and never said a cross word, and even when they drowned his pet cat in the well, let out his pigs, turned the old cow in his garden and stoned all his young Plymouth Rock chickens to death, he just said, "Poor little fellars, they hain't got no mother now," and he guessed they didn't mean any harm, and took care of them till a relative came and took them away.

We figured all these things up and made up our minds that no fair-minded God would send a great, big-hearted, innocent cowman, who never harmed anybody in his life, to a place like hell was supposed to be. Even if God couldn't let him into heaven on 'count of his wearing his pants in his boots, eating with his knife at the table place of his fork, drinking his coffee out his saucer and other ignorant ways, yet He might give him a pretty decent place away out where there wasn't any sheepmen, and if He didn't have somebody handy to keep old Chuck company just let him have a deck or two of cards to play solitaire with and Chuck wouldn't mind.

Old Chuckwagon was mighty fond of white-faced cattle, and just as he breathed his last he sorter roused up and stretched out his arms, with his eyes as bright as 'lectric lamps, and said: "Boys, I see another country, just lots of big grass, with running streams of water, big herds of white-face cattle, and they are all mavericks, not a brand on 'em, and not a sheep-wagon in sight." And them was his last words.

He lay on the sidetrack, poor honest Chuckwagon,
　The pallor of death creeping fast o'er his brow;
Said he to the cowboys, "My rope is a dragging,
　I'm going o'er the divide and going right now.

"I've often faced death with the bronks and the cattle,
　And meeting him now doesn't take so much sand.
For sooner or later with death all must grapple,
　And all that we need is to show a straight brand.

"I would like one more glimpse at the side of the mountain,
　Before I saddle up for Eternity's divide;
The ranch house, the meadow, the spring like a fountain,
　But, alas for poor Chuck, my feet are hogtied."

Down his bronzed hardy cheeks the warm tears were
　stealing,
　At the memory of his cow ranch, so pleasant and bright.
A smile like an angel played over each feature,
　And the soul of the cowboy rode out of sight.

CHAPTER X.

THE DISAPPEARANCE OF THE SHEEPMEN.

After we buried Chuckwagon we walked across a bend in the road and caught up with the stock train and strolled on ahead with sad hearts and silent lips till we arrived at the top of Sherman Hill. We prepared to wait for the arrival of the stock train, so selecting a site on the south side of Ames monument, we built a snow hut by rolling up huge snowballs and piling them up one on top of the other for walls to a height of about seven and one-half feet, leaving a space for our room of about twelve feet square inside, and gradually drawing them together at the top for a roof, and making a big snowball for the door. After it was all finished we let the sheepmen and Jackdo go over across the canyon about two miles and build another hut for themselves. We moved our luggage (which we had carried to lighten up the train) inside, and after closing the door with the big snowball, we ate a hearty supper of boiled rawhide, and spreading

67

down a sheet of mist, we rolled up in a blanket of fog and went to sleep.

We hadn't no more than got to sleep before a lightning rod agent by the name of Woods came along and put up lightning rods all over our snow hut and woke us up to sign $350 worth of notes for the rods. This matter attended to, we went to sleep again and the lightning rod agent went over across the canyon to the sheepmen's hut and put rods on it. This man Woods was a good fellar, got people to sign notes by the wholesale, but never did anything so low as to collect them, just turned them over to a lawyer and let him attend to that. He was always broke and borrowed your last "five" in a way that endeared him to you for life. He never bothered with paying for anything, always said, "Just put it down, or charge it," in such a lofty way that everyone in hearing would begin to hunt for pencils right off. He put lightning rods on everything, even to prairie dogs' houses and ant heaps, took anybody's note with any kind of signature.

Cottswool Canvasback, Rambolet Bill and Jackdo couldn't write, but he had Rambolet Bill make his mark to the note and then Cottswool Canvasback and

Jackdo witnessed it by affixing their mark; then he had Cottswool Canvasback sign his mark as security and Rambolet Bill and Jackdo witness the signature with their marks; then had Jackdo sign his mark as security and Rambolet and Cottswool witness it with their marks.

We had put out a signal flag on our snow hut so the trainmen would know where to find us when they came along with the stock. When we awoke next morning and went outdoors a strange sight greeted our astonished vision. There had come a *chinook wind in the night and melted the snow off up to within one hundred feet of our altitude. As Jackdo and the two sheepmen had built their snow residence about 150 feet lower altitude on the other side of the canyon, their house had melted down over their heads, and as they were nowhere in sight it was safe to presume they had been carried away in the ruins. We had quite an argument now, whether we should try to find them or not. Dillbery Ike maintained they was human beings and as such was entitled to our looking for them. Packsaddle Jack said he didn't know

*For the benefit of our readers who do not know what a chinook wind is, I will explain that it is a hot, violent coast wind which blows at certain periods of the year at certain altitudes in the West.

for sure whether sheepmen were humans or not. He guessed it was a mighty broad word and covered a heap of things. Eatumup Jake said he reckoned they would turn up all right, that sheepmen didn't die very easy, that he knowed them to pack off more lead than an antelope would and still live; he guessed being washed off the side of the mountain wouldn't kill them. He said we'd better wait till the trainmen came along and then report the matter to them, as the sheepmen would want damages off the railroad or somebody and we'd better not hunt them up too quick as it might jeopardize their case. We all agreed there was some difference in sheepmen, and that Rambolet Bill and Cottswool Canvasback certainly belonged to the better class, and we all fell to telling stories of the generous, open-handed things that sheepmen of our acquaintance had done.

Packsaddle Jack said he knowed a sheepman once by the name of Black Face, who was so good-hearted that he paid $20 towards one of his herder's doctor bill when he lost both feet by their being frozen in the great Wyoming blizzard in '94. The herder stayed with the sheep for seventy-two hours in the Bad Lands and saved all the 3,000 head except seven, that got over the bank of the creek into ice and water and drowned. The herder having got all but these seven head out and getting his feet wet they froze so hard that Black Face said his feet was rattling together like rocks when he found him still herding the sheep. Of course, the sheep might have all perished in the storm if the herder didn't stay with them, and of course, the herder didn't have anything to eat the entire three days in the storm, as he was miles from any habitation and that way saved Black Face 30 cents in grub. But we all agreed that while Black Face would feel the greatest anguish at the loss of the seven sheep and giving up the $20, yet the satisfaction of doing a generous deed and the pride he would experience when it was mentioned in the item column of the local county paper would partially alleviate that anguish.

Eatumup Jake said he knew a sheepman by the name of Hatchet Face from Connecticut, who had sheep ranches out there in Utah, and he was so kindhearted that when one of his herders kept his sheep in a widow neighbor's field till they ate up everything in sight, even her lawn and flower garden, he apologized to the widow when she returned from nursing

a poor family through a spell of sickness, and told her
he would pay her something, and while he never did
pay her anything, yet he always seemed sorry, while
a lot of sheepmen would have laid awake nights to
have studied a way how to eat out the widow again.
Eatumup Jake said old Hatchet Face, when he prayed
in church Sundays (he being a strict Presbyterian), he
always prayed for the poor and widows and orphans,
and that showed he had a good heart, to use what influence he had with God Almighty and get Him to do
something for widows and orphans and poor people.

Dillbery Ike said he knew a sheepman by the
name of Shearclose, and while he never gave his
hired help any meat to eat except old broken-mouthed
ewes in the winter and dead lambs in the spring and
summer, and herded his sheep around homesteaders'
little ranches till their milk cows mighty near starved
to death, yet old Shearclose gave $5 for a ticket to
a charity ball once when a list of the names of all the
people who bought tickets was printed in the county paper.

After we summed all these things up, our hearts
got so warm thinking of these acts of generosity by
sheepmen that we concluded to make a hunt for Ram-

C. J. Lane, General Freight Agent and Pass Distributer to Live Stock Shippers.

bolet Bill, Cottswool Canvasback and Jackdo. We
now discussed a great many plans how to rescue
them. While we were arguing the stock train came,
and when we told the conductor, he immediately had
the agent wire General Freight Agent C. J. Lane at
Omaha the following message:

"Two prominent sheepmen swept away by fresh-
et while camping ahead of special stock train No.
79531. Please wire instructions how to find them."

Lane immediately wired back not to find them,
and if there was any trace left of them to obliterate
it at once.

JACKDO'S STORY OF HIS ESCAPE.

We now sauntered down Sherman Hill ahead of
the train to Cheyenne, expecting to get some help
there to find Rambolet Bill and Cottswool Canvasback, and was much surprised to discover Jackdo
asleep riding on the trucks of a car in a special that
went by, and on waking him up he told us the following story of his escape:

He said when the flood came he got astride a big
snowball and making a compass out of a piece of
lightning rod he pointed it for the north star so as to

not lose his bearings and started for Cheyenne. He said it was a wild ride, that he passed cattle and horses, forests and ranches in quick succession and his snowball was almost worn out when he got below the altitude of the chinook wind and struck a country of ice and snow again. But it was impossible to stop, he had acquired such a momentum going down the mountain that he slid through nine miles of cactus and prickly pears without having changed the sitting position he started in. However, after his snowball wore out, he just held up his feet and kept on till he struck a special stock train going East, and after knocking two of the cars off the rails and breaking the bumpers of a half-dozen more, he checked up enough to crawl on a brake beam and go to sleep. He knew nothing of Rambolet Bill and Cottswool Canvasback.

CHAPTER XI.

OUR ARRIVAL IN CHEYENNE.

We arrived in Cheyenne, and after reporting to the dispatcher what time our special stock train would arrive, we exposed Jackdo to the gentle breeze, which is always on tap in Cheyenne, and it blew all the cactus slivers out of his anatomy that he had accumulated in his nine miles slide in just thirteen seconds. We then started out to see the town. We asked an expressman on the corner of Main Street— he was the only live human being in sight—what was the main features of Cheyenne. He said Tom Horn and Senator Warren. We asked him what they was noted for, and he said that Tom Horn was noted for killing people that took things that didn't belong to them and then blowing his horn about it afterwards, and Senator Warren was noted for building wire fences on government land and taking everything in sight.

Not seeing anyone on the streets, we asked him

if it was Sunday, and he said every day was Sunday in Cheyenne except when they had a political rally, and then it was a durn Democratic funeral from sun to sun, burying the Democratic party over and over again, they rehearsed them same old services. Whenever people saw the politicians on the streets with clean shirts on they knew the Democratic party was going to have another funeral. The folks in Cheyenne was always going to church, or else burying the Democratic party. We asked him what the prevailing religion of the town was, and he said, "High-priced wool."

Just then Senator W—— came along, and hearing of the disappearance of two sheepmen, and it being near election time, he immediately had all the troops called out, got together a vast army of United States deputy marshals and wired the president of the Overland, who immediately chartered a special train loaded with detectives, and two cars loaded with blood-hounds in charge of a lawyer by the name of Ashby from Lincoln; one car loaded with automobiles, two cars loaded with bottled goods and other useful supplies and two pianos with pianola attachments, seven trunks full of mechanical music in air-tight bottles, and one steam calliope near the engine on a flat car. The Governor of Wyoming met the special train at Cheyenne, and after issuing a proclamation offering a large reward for the sheepmen dead or alive, joined the U. P. president in his car. They now started the steam calliope, and the Governor playing one of the pianola-attachment pianos, the U. P. president playing the other. The state chairman of the Republican party sang the old familiar hymn, "Ninety and Nine Were Safely Laid in the Shelter of the Fold," and Senator W———— made a speech something like this:

He said: "Fellow sheepmen and what few other citizens there are in Wyoming: What's the matter with the sheep business? Have we deteriorated in the eyes of the world in the last two thousand years? Who writes poetry of the sheep and sheepherder of the present time? What artist puts priceless paintings on canvass of the sheep business to-day? Why, fellow sheepmen, in ancient times all the poetry that was written was of the shepherd and his flock, and in every palace, in the most conspicuous place, was a picture of a tall shepherd with venerable beard and flowing locks, with his serape thrown carelessly over

—6

his shoulder, a long shepherd's crook in his hand, lead
ing his sheep over the hill into some fresher pasture.
And when the people saw the original of this painting
in ye ancient time appearing over the hill in the sun-
set glow, they cried: 'Lo, behold the shepherd cometh.'
Now what do they say? This is what you hear: 'Well,
look at that lousy sheepherding scoundrel coming over
the divide with his sheep. Boys, get your black masks
and the wagon spokes.'

"Now," he says, "wouldn't that Ram you? What
would our party have amounted to in Wyoming if I
hadn't Bucked everything in sight? I've Lambed the
stuffing out of the Democrats and Pulled Wool over
the eyes of the would-be party leaders till we have
Pretty Good Grazing and Fair We(a)thers.

"In a few days we will be called on to decide a
great question at the polls, whether Billy Bryan will
build your house out of cold, clammy, frosty silver
bricks, or whether we will have houses built out of all
wool. You must make a choice between the two. If
you vote for me, it means a good, warm woolen house,
good woolen underclothes, good woolen overclothes."

Judge Carey tried to say something about a gold
plank, but everybody frowned at him so that he slunk

off in the crowd and shortly afterwards was seen in a back alley having a heart-to-heart talk with two bow-legged cowpunchers who, while they did not know much about any kind of gold, let alone a big gold standard, knew anything was better than all this talk about sheep and wool.

Senator W——— kept talking as long as he could keep the Governor and the U. P. president making music. He said everybody who voted right could sit on his right hand with the sheep, otherwise they would have to associate with the goats on his left that was herded by Billy Bryan. Some of the crowd grumbled about associating with either one, but the Senator said there was no choice if they stayed in Wyoming.

A carriage now dashed up, all emblazoned with a coat-of-arms, which consisted of a panel of barbed wire fence with a rampant sheep leaning against it. The Senator entered this carriage, rolled away and the crowd followed him.

Although there had been no effort made to find the sheepmen, yet apparently the object of the railroad expedition had been accomplished, and they were about to return when they discovered that three of the highest-priced detectives were missing. They were found almost immediately on the trail of the man who could tell why a life-long Democrat in Wyoming, as soon as he starts in the sheep business, gets a public office in place of a life-long Republican who didn't own any sheep. The detectives were called off the trail and the president of the great Overland began his return. We heard afterwards that Captain Ashby claimed that two of the most valuable blood-hounds escaped from the hound car and he demanded that the U. P. pay him $700 for the dogs. He claimed that if they struck the trail of anything they would follow it to the death. A couple of mangy fox-hounds were found dead in an alley back of one of the Cheyenne hotels the next morning after the president's train left, and as it was known that one of the hotel cooks had been down to the train, these were supposed to be the dogs, and the claim was allowed. What caused their death was a matter of conjecture. There was quite a pile of hotel grub laying near the dogs. The hotel boarders differed in opinion. Some said the dogs died of indigestion and some said of starvation.

CHAPTER XII.

The Post-Hole Digger's Ghost.

The skeletons of Rambolet Bill and Cottswool Canvasback were found a long time after this all happened by one of the Warren Live Stock Company's fence riders. This fence commences in northeastern Colorado near the 27th degree of longitude west from Washington, and extends west over hills and valleys, plains and mountains, through all kinds of latitudes, longitudes and vicissitudes. There is a legend in regard to the building of this fence that is told in whispers when the fire burns low of a night in western homes. It runs something like this:

Years ago Senator Warren, Manager Gleason and some other Massachusetts Yankees started in the sheep business in southern Wyoming and northern Colorado, and as the country was large they thought it would be a good thing to fence in a few hundred thousand acres of government land and save the grass so fenced in case of hard winters and other things and

83

graze their sheep in this enclosure only when there was no more grass around the little homesteads taken here and there by settlers. So hiring a young German from the Old Country, who couldn't speak a word of English, to dig the post-holes, they got him a brand-new shovel, a post-bar about eight feet long, the famous receipt for cooking jackrabbits, and started him digging near the 27th degree of longitude west from Washington. Pointing toward the setting sun in the west, they went off and left him. The German was never seen alive again, but he left a never-ending line of post-holes behind him. The Warren Live Stock Company, it is said, put on a great many men setting the posts in these holes and stringing barbed wire on them, and although they kept ever increasing the force that built the fence, yet they never caught up with the German, and time after time the post-setters would come to the top of a high hill or a range of mountains and thought they would come in sight of the German, only to see a long line of post-holes stretching away over hill and valley towards the setting sun.

After a while the Mormons along the line of Utah and Wyoming complained of seeing a ghost about the time they drove their cows home of an evening. They said it was a German with grizzled locks and flowing beard, with a large meerschaum pipe in his mouth and a shovel in one hand from which the blade was worn down to the handle and a post-bar no bigger than a drag tooth in the other hand. He was always looking toward the setting sun, shading his eyes with his hand and muttering these words: "Das sinkende Sonne, ich fange sie nicht."

But when they approached close to him, or spoke to him, he immediately vanished. When the ghost wasn't disturbed it seemed to be digging holes. It would go through the motions of digging a hole in the ground, then rising up, take thirteen steps in a westerly direction, look back to see if the line was straight, dig another hole, and go on. Sometimes the ghost seemed to be studying a well-worn piece of paper, which was undoubtedly the receipt for cooking jackrabbits, and would mutter in German, "O wohene, O wohene ist er gegangen, mit Schwanz so kurz und Ohr so lang? O wohene ist mein Hase gegangen?"

After awhile the ghost began to appear in western Utah and still later on in Nevada, always digging a never-ending imaginary line of post-holes. No one never knew where the actual post-holes left off and the imaginary ones commenced.

As the Routt County cattlemen in western Colorado never allowed any sheepmen to encroach on their
range, and they always killed all the sheep and sheepmen who dared to intrude, of course, the Warren Live
Stock had to stop building fence west and turn north
before they got there.

When the ghastly skeletons of Rambolet Bill and
Cottswool Canvasback were found lying by this fence,
their bones picked clean by coyotes and vultures, a
small book was picked up near them which proved to
be a diary of their adventures and last hours of suffering. It will be remembered that Rambolet Bill and
Cottswool Canvasback couldn't write, but they had
drawn pictures in the book, and when we had gotten
another sheepman who couldn't write to examine them
he read them just like print. The first picture was a
mountain with a lot of marks, which was interpreted
as the flood, and two men drawn crosswise laying
down was the sheepmen being washed away. The
next picture was a wire fence with two men clinging
to it. He said that was when they washed into the
fence. The next was another fence picture showing
two men walking along it. There was about fifty
pictures after this one, but they always had a section

of a wire fence in them. Several pictures in the front part of the book showed the two men eating jackrabbits, but later on some of the pictures showed them chasing a prairie dog, or trying to slip up on one, indicating that they couldn't find any more jackrabbits. There was pictures of them chewing bits of their clothes to get the sheep grease out of them. Then there was pictures of them pointing to their mouths and stomachs, finally in the last picture they were in the act of eating a piece of paper with some writing on it, which was probably the receipt for cooking jackrabbits. They probably had walked hundreds of miles along this fence before they finally succumbed, and as it was a country where they had herded large bands of sheep the grass had become so exterminated that no jackrabbits could live there, and consequently Rambolet Bill and Cottswool Canvasback had gradually starved to death.

Two guileless sheepmen lay sleeping on the side of a barren
    hill,
One's name was Cottswool Canvasback, the other was Rambo-
    bolet Bill.
They were dreaming, sweetly dreaming, the fore part of the
    night
Of grazing their sheep on a homesteader's claim when he was
    out of sight.

But hark! to the wind that's rising; 'tis coming fast and
    warm;
Little recked the sleepers that it would do them harm;
But the roar was growing louder, as the pine trees bent and
    shook,
And the birds were screaming loudly, "Beware of the warm
    chinook."

When that hot blast struck their hut, built out of walls of snow,
That house turned into a river in a way that wasn't slow;
Washed off these dreaming sheepmen in the middle of the
    night.
As the waters swept the dreamers away, what must have been
    their fright,

Till tangled up in Warren's fence that's built o'er mountain
    and vale,
They followed it the rest of their lives, winding o'er hill and
    dale.
When found by the annual fence rider, they long since had
    been dead,
Their bones picked clean by coyotes, with vultures hovering
    o'erhead.

CHAPTER XIII.

GRAFTING.

One night while we were in Cheyenne we were going from the dispatcher's office down to our way-car, which was, as usual, about one mile from the depot. The railroad company had quite a number of police on duty in the yards to watch for strikers, there having been a machinists' strike on for a long time. No strikers had ever come around the railroad yards nights or even interfered with any one at any time, but a lot of fellows who wanted soft jobs as watchmen made the officials of the road think the strikers were going to do something, and these night watchmen had, it seems, been looking for a long time for some weak tramp to beat to death and then claim the tramp was working in the interest of the strikers and was about to injure railroad property when those awful sleuths caught him in the act and put his light out. Thus they could get a fresh hold on their jobs. However, they had been unable to catch a tramp, and as they had to get somebody in order to hold their jobs, they cornered Dillbery Ike, who had loitered behind the rest, and one of the valiant watchmen swiping him over the head with a six-shooter, scalped him as clean as a Sioux Injun would have done it with a scalping knife. Hearing Dillbery Ike's cries for help, we went to his rescue, and none too soon, as the watchman was still beating him. When we had got a doctor for Dillbery, of course the first thing he asked for was Dillbery's scalp, so he could sew it on again. But although we made a long search for the scalp, we only found a few bloody hairs, and undoubtedly some hungry canine prowling around had ate it up. However, the railroad company, after some parleying, agreed to pay for having a new one grafted on, and as grafting is the long suit of the Cheyenne doctors, there was a general scramble for the job. 'Twas finally agreed to divide the job amongst them, or rather divide the space and the money. The doctors immediately advertised for contributions of pieces of scalp to graft on Dillbery's head, but no one responding they offered to buy some sections of scalp, and this ad was responded to in a mysterious way by a midnight visitor at each of their offices, with a small

Dillbery Ike as a Shipper.

piece of very close shaven fresh scalp, which the visitor (who was a woman in each case and so muffled up that her features couldn't be seen) claimed she had cut off Billy's or Johnny's or Jimmy's head after putting them under the influence of ether.

Each of the four doctors paid her $25 and hiked off to plaster the piece of hide on Dillbery Ike's cranium. The scalped place had been carefully laid off by a civil engineer, so each of the four doctors knew his corner in the block, and without any courtesies to one another they each trimmed down his $25 piece of hide to fit his corner and then fastened it on. The grafting took at once and in a few days was healed over nicely, despite the fact it turned out that the woman had taken a different piece of scalp off from different pet animals which she kept. One was a pet pig, another a pet goat, another a pet sheep and the fourth a pet dog of the Newfoundland breed. When the hair, wool and bristles all began to make a luxuriant growth on Dillbery's new scalp, he seemed to be more or less affected by the dispositions of each animal from which a part of the wonderful scalp was removed, and when the different colored hair, wool and bristles had grown to a good length the effect of this unique head covering was very striking to strangers. However, Dillbery lke was justly proud of it, as the doctors had charged the Union Pacific $1,200 for this variegated scalp. Of course, no other cowpuncher could boast of such a valuable head covering.

There was one little white bare spot in the center which was above timber line, as it were, where the doctors, making these four corners, had each been a little shy of material, and here was a little open, or park, on the top of his head in which sheep ticks, hog lice, dog fleas and goat vermin could have a common ground to assemble and sun themselves in.

CHAPTER XIV.

THE FILE.

After learning the fate of the two sheepmen we prepared to leave Cheyenne and catch up with our stock train, which we figured would take us a day or so. We interviewed the dispatcher, superintendent and station agent at Cheyenne, asking each one of them to wire down the road and see if they could locate the special. Every one of them wired and the next day about noon the agent got word the stock was at Egbert. That evening the superintendent got a message that they was between Egbert and Pine Bluffs. About midnight the dispatcher got a message that they were hourly expected in Pine Bluffs, so we started on to overtake them.

We had noticed with a great deal of anxiety that the wrinkles had commenced to accumulate on our cattle's horns, as a new wrinkle grows each year after an animal is two years old, and we had been advised by several cattlemen who had been in the habit of

95

taking their cattle by rail to market in place of driving them, to procure files and rasps and remove these
wrinkles before we got to Omaha. So we secured a
lot of rasps and files at Cheyenne and had Jackdo car-
ry them for us, and when we caught up with the train
we went to work to take off the sign of old age which
had come on our stock since shipping them, as the
Nebraska corn-raisers only want young stock to feed
When we first loaded our cattle we were informed
that they were a little bit too fat for the killers, but, of
course, the next day, they was about four pounds too
thin for the killers, but too fat for the feeders. However, by this time they were nothing but petrified
skeletons, and Dillbery Ike wanted to leave the
wrinkles on their horns and sell the entire outfit for
antiques. But the more we discussed it, the more
we made up our minds that as this railroad done a
large business hauling stock, the antique cattle market must be overstocked. So we finally concluded to
take off the wrinkles that had grown since we started
and sell the cattle on their merits. We arranged to
run two day shifts and one night shift of six hours
each and to commence up next the engine and work
back. So getting in the first car we climbed astride

the critters' necks and commenced to file. Day after day, night after night, we kept at this wearisome task, and when our files and rasps became worn we sent Jackdo (who wouldn't work, but who didn't mind tramping) to the nearest town to get fresh files and rasps. Sometimes we became discouraged when we saw the wrinkles starting again that we had removed to commence with, and our eyes filled with bitter tears when we thought how much better it would have been to have trailed our cattle through, or even sold them to some Nebraska sucker and taken his draft on a commission house. Dillbery Ike, who had some education, made up a song for us to sing while we were at work, called "The Song of the File," and one of us would sing a verse and then all join in the chorus, and this song helped us a great deal. Here it is:

Oh! we are a bunch of cattlemen,
Going to market with our stock again,
And, as we ship over a road that's bum,
The days they go and the days they come.

Chorus.

Cheer up, brave hearts, and list to the file
As the wrinkles keep dropping below in a pile;
Never fear, my boys, we have plenty of time
To remove old age that's known by the wrinkle sign.

And as time goes by the wrinkles grow
On the horns of the cattl. in a train that's slow;
For every year after the second a cow that's born
Another wrinkle grows upon each horn.

While we have a job that isn't so soft,
A-trying to rasp these wrinkles off,
To make their horns look smooth and bright,
We file all day and we file all night.

And as we file, we whistle and sing,
Trying to make it a jolly thing,
To remove the wrinkles that are sure to grow
On the horns of cattle with a road that's slow.

Astride their necks, we sit and file,
And through our tears, we try to smile.
Cheer up, brave hearts, cheer up, we say again,
As we camp along with the bum stock train.

CHAPTER XV.

THE CATTLE STAMPEDE.

The boys all got to talking about stampedes one night while we were waiting on a sidetrack, and I related to them an experience of my own.

A number of years ago, I bought some 15,000 steers in southern Arizona, and shipping them to Denver, Colorado, divided them up into herds of about 3,500 head in each herd and started to trail these herds north to Wyoming. About 4,000 head of these steers were from 4 to 10 years old and were known as outlaws in the country where they were raised. These steers were almost as wild as elk; very tall, thin, rawboned, high-headed, with enormous horns and long tails, and as there was great danger of their stampeding at any time, I put all of them in a herd by themselves and went with that herd myself. I worried about these steers night and day, and talked to my men incessantly about how to handle them and what to do if the cattle stampeded. There is only one thing

to do in case of a stampede of a herd of wild range
steers, and that is for every cowboy to get in the lead
of them with a good horse and keep in the lead without trying to stop them, but gradually turn them
and get them to running in a circle, or "milling," as
it is commonly known among cowboys. Cattle on the
trail never stampede but one way, and that is back
the way they come from. If you can succeed in turning them in some other direction, you can gradually
bring them to a stop. These long-legged range steers
can run almost as fast as the swiftest horse.

So we kept our best and swiftest horses saddled
all night, ready to spring onto in case the herd ever
got started. We were driving in a northerly direction
all the time, and every night took the herd fully a
mile north of the mess wagon camp before we bedded
them down. I had fourteen men in the outfit, half of
them old-time cowboys and the other half would-be
cowboys; several of them what we used to call tenderfeet.

Amongst the green hands at trailing cattle was
the nephew of my eastern partner, a college-bred boy,
with blonde, curly hair and a face as merry as a girl's
at a May day picnic. The boys all called him Curley.

He was as lovable a lad as I ever met, but positively refused to take this enormous herd of old outlaw, long-horned steers as a serious proposition.

We had always four men on night herd at a time, each gang standing night guard three hours, when they were relieved by another four men. The first gang was 8 to 11 o'clock in the evening; the next 11 till 2 and the last guard stood from 2 till daylight, and then started the herd traveling north again. I kept two old cow hands and two green ones on each guard, and had been nine days on the trail; had traveled about a hundred miles without any mishap. We had bright moonlight nights. The grass was fine, being about the first of June, and I was beginning to feel a little easier, when one night we were camped on a high rolling prairie near the Wyoming line.

Curley and three other men had just went on guard at 2 o'clock in the morning. The moon was shining bright as day. Everything was as still as could be, the old long-horned outlaws all lying down sleeping, probably dreaming of the cactus-covered hillsides in their old home in Arizona. Curley was on the north side of the herd and rolling a cigarette. He forgot my oft-repeated injunction not to light a parlor match around the herd in the night, but scratched one on his saddle horn. When that match popped, there was a roar like an earthquake and the herd was gone in the wink of an eyelid; just two minutes from the time Curley scratched his match, that wild, crazy avalanche of cattle was running over that camp outfit, two and three deep. But at that first roar, I was out of my blankets. running for my hoss and hollering, "Come on, boys!" with a rising inflection on "boys." The old hands knew what was coming and were on their hosses soon as I was, but the tenderfeet stampeded their own hosses trying to get onto them, and their hosses all got away except two, and when their riders finally got on them, they took across the hills as fast as they could go out the way of that horde of on-coming wild-eyed demons. The men who lost their hosses crawled under the front end of the big heavy roundup wagon, and for a wonder the herd didn't over-turn the wagon, although lots of them broke their horns on it and some broke their legs. When I lit in the saddle, and looked around, five of my cowboys was lined up side of me, their hosses jumping and snort-ing, for them old cow hosses scented the danger and I only had time to say, "Keep cool; hold your hosses'

The Stampede

heads high, boys, and keep two hundred yards ahead of the cattle for at least five miles. If your hoss gives out try to get off to one side," and then that earthquake (as one of the tenderfeet called it when he first woke up) was at our heels, and we were riding for our own lives as well as to stop the cattle, because if a hoss stumbled or stepped in a badger hole there wouldn't be even a semblance of his rider left after those thousands of hoofs had got through pounding him. I was riding a Blackhawk Morgan hoss with wonderful speed and endurance and very sure footed, which was the main thing, and I allowed the herd to get up in a hundred yards of me, and seeing the country was comparatively smooth ahead of me, I turned in my saddle and looked back at the cattle.

I had been in stampedes before, but nothing like this. The cattle were running their best, all the cripples and drags in the lead, their sore feet forgotten. Every steer had his long tail in the air, and those 4,000 waving tails made me think of a sudden whirlwind in a forest of young timber. Once in a while I could see a little ripple in the sea of shining backs, and I knew a steer had stumbled and gone down and his fellows had tramped him into mincemeat as they went over

him. They were constantly breaking one another's
big horns as they clashed and crowded together, and
1 could hear their horns striking and breaking above
the roar of the thousands of hoofs on the hard ground.

As my eyes moved over the herd and to one side,
I caught sight of a rider on a grey hoss, using whip
and spur, trying to get ahead of the cattle, and I
knew at a glance it was Curley, as none of the other
boys had a grey hoss that night. I could see he was
slowly forging ahead and getting nearer the lead of
the cattle all the time.

We had gone about ten or twelve miles and had
left the smooth, rolling prairie behind us and were
thundering down the divide on to the broken country
along Crow Creek. Now, cattle on a stampede all follow the leaders, and after I and my half dozen cowboys had ridden in the lead of that herd for twelve or
fifteen miles, gradually letting the cattle get close to
us, but none by us, why we were the leaders, and when
we began to strike that rough ground, my cowboys
gradually veered to the left, so as to lead the herd
away from the creek and onto the divide again. But
Curley was on the left side of the herd. None of the
other boys had noticed him, and when the herd began

to swerve to the left, it put him on the inside of a quarter moon of rushing, roaring cattle. I hollered and screamed to my men, but in that awful roar could hardly hear my own voice, let alone make my men hear me, and just then we went down into a steep gulch and up the other side. I saw the hind end of the herd sweep across from their course of the quarter circle towards the leaders, saw the grey hoss and Curley go over the bank of the gulch out of sight amidst hordes of struggling animals. But as I looked back at the cattle swarming up the other bank I looked in vain for that grey hoss and his curly-haired rider. Sick at heart, I thought of what was lying in the bottom of that gulch in place of the sunny-haired boy my partner had sent out to me, and I wished that eighty thousand dollars worth of hides, horns and hoofs that was still thundering on behind was back in the cactus forests of Arizona.

As the herd swung out on the divide they split in two, part of them turning to the left, making a circle of about two miles, myself and two cowboys heading this part of the herd and keeping them running in a smaller circle all the time till they stopped. The other part of the herd kept on for about five miles further, then they split in two, and the cowboys divided and finally got both bunches stopped; not, however, till one bunch had gone about ten miles beyond where I had got the first herd quieted.

It was now broad daylight, and I started back to the gulch where poor Curley had disappeared. When I came in sight of the gulch, I saw his dead hoss, trampled into an unrecognizable mass, lying in the bottom of the gulch, but could see nothing of Curley. While gazing up and down the gulch which was over-hung with rocks in places, I heard someone whistling a tune, and looking in that direction, saw Curley with his back to me, perched on a rock whistling as merry as a bird.

He told me that as his hoss tumbled over the rocky bank, he fell off into a crevice, and crawling back under the rocks, he watched the procession go over him.

We were three days getting the cattle back to where they had started and two hundred of them were dead or had to be shot, and hundreds had their horns broken off and hanging by slivers. It had cost in dead cattle and damage to the living at least $10,000. But I was so glad to get that curly-headed scamp back alive and unhurt I never said a word to him.

CHAPTER XVI.

CATCHING A MAVERICK.

One day while waiting for a gravel train going west, we all got to talking about catching mavericks. Eatumup Jake said he'd always been too honest to go out on the range and hunt mavericks; Dillbery Ike said he was too, but he wasn't so durned honest as to let a maverick chase him out of his own corral; and they asked me what I thought about branding mavericks. I told them that I thought it was a bad practice to hunt mavericks all the time, but whenever a maverick came around hunting me up, I generally built a fire and put a branding iron in to heat. But I told them I would always remember one maverick I had an adventure with, and after they had all promised me not to ever tell the story to any one, I told them the following:

One hot day in the spring of '84 I started across the hills from my ranch to town, fifteen miles away. I generally had a good riata on my saddle, but this day, for some reason, I didn't take anything but a piece of rope fifteen feet long. I didn't expect to meet any mavericks, as it was just after the spring round up and there wasn't a chance in a hundred of seeing one. My way was across a high, broken country, without a house or a ranch the entire distance. There was bunches of cattle and horses everywhere eating the luxuriant grass, drinking out of the clear running streams of mountain water or lying down too full to eat or drink any more. I was riding one of my best hosses, as everybody did when they went to town; had my high-heeled boots blacked till you could see your face in them; was wearing a brand-new $12 Stetson hat that was made to order; had on a pair of new California pants—they were sort of a lavender color with checks an inch square, and I was more than proud of them. I had on a white silk shirt and a blue silk handkerchief round my neck, a red silk vest with black polka dots on it, but didn't have any coat to match this brilliant costume, so was in my shirt sleeves.

I rode along, setting kind of side ways, my hat cocked over my ear, a-looking down at myself from time to time, and I was about the most self-satisfied cowpuncher ever was, didn't envy a saloon-keeper in the territory, and saloon-keepers had as much influence in Wyoming them days as a sheepman does now, and that's saying all you can say, when it's known that the sheepmen to-day in Wyoming fill almost every office, elective and appointive.

Well I had got about half way to town and was a-studying 'bout a girl I bid goodbye to in the East fifteen years before, and sort a-wishing she could see me now, when all of a sudden I looked up and right there, not fifty feet away, was a big, fat, black bull maverick. He was about a year and a half old and would weigh 800 pounds. He was wild as an elk and had given a loud snuff on seeing me, which had called my attention to him. I immediately commenced making that short piece of rope into a lasso. There wasn't much more than enough for the loop, but I knew old Bill, the hoss I was riding, could catch him on any kind of ground, so throwed the spurs in and went sailing over the breaks and coolies after that wild bull maverick. I soon caught up with him, but found it amost impossible to throw the loop over his head with such a short rope, as he dodged to one side or the other every time I got in reach. However, I

8—

finally got it over his horns just as he went over a bank, but before I could take any *dallys, he jerked the rope out of my hands and was gone with it.

Now I had got to pick up the rope, and as it only dragged five or six feet behind him, I would have to ride by him and grab the rope near his head as I went by: but he was still on the dodge, and I made several passes at it and missed. The bull was getting mad by this time, and lowering his head and elevating his tail he soon had me on the dodge. Whenever I wasn't chasing the bull, he was chasing me. Thus we had it up one gulch and down another. Many times I grabbed the rope only to have it jerked out of my fingers, but finally got a wrap around my saddle horn and a knot tied. It never had occurred to me I couldn't throw him with that short rope till I was tied hard and fast to him and riding down the gulch at breakneck speed with that black bull a close second.

We had been chasing each other now for over an hour and my hoss was getting tired, but Mr. Bull seemed to be fresher than ever. I had lost my new Stetson hat early in the game, and, as we had soused through a good many alkali mud-holes, I was spat-

---

*Wrapping rope around the saddle horn.

tered from head to foot with mud. My white silk shirt and lavender-colored pants were a total wreck. But something had got to be done, and watching the bull till he was veering a little to the left of my hoss I made a quick turn to the right, and stopping right quick, turned Mr. Bull over on his back. Before he could get up I was off and on top of him, had his tail between his hind legs, my knees in his flank, and, as every cowpuncher knows, I could hold him down. My hoss was pulling on the rope same as any well-trained cow hoss would, keeping the bull's head stretched out, and there wasn't the least possible show of him getting up; but as I didn't have any short foot ropes to tie his feet with, I just had to set in his flank and keep tight hold of his tail. Billy, my hoss, had got hot and excited during the race and kept surging on the rope more than was necessary. I kept saying, "Whoa, Bill," but directly he give an extra hard pull, the rope broke right at the bull's head, and despite my nice talk, Billy turned his back to me and started across the hills for home. In vain I hollered, "Whoa, Bill; come, Billy," he never looked around but once, and that was just as he disappeared over the hill. He sort a-looked back for a moment, as much as to say, "Well you wanted that darn little black bull so bad, now you got him stay with him," and that's what I had to do. He was twice as hard to hold now without any rope on his head, but I knew if he ever got up, he would gore me to death, as there wasn't a tree or rock to get behind.

It was about noon. The hot sun was pouring down on my bare head and I was choking with thirst. No one ever traveled that way but me. Miles away to any habitation, there I would have to stay in that stooping position, holding on to that little black bull's tail. I was young and strong, but my back began to ache, my hand would cramp clasping that bull's tail so tightly, but still I held on somehow, for I knew certain death awaited me if I let go. A bunch of cattle came along and circled around me with wide-eyed astonishment, then trotted off; a couple of antelope came running over the hill, and catching sight of me in that ridiculous position, their curiosity overcame their timidity and they kept getting nearer and nearer, till only a few rods away, the old buck antelope stopped and snuffed very loudly and stamped with his fore feet, but, not being able to get any response out of the black bull and me, finally left. Then a

Catching a Maverick.

silly jackrabbit came hopping up on three legs, and after standing up several times on his hind legs as high as possible and pulling his whiskers some, he shook his big ears as much as to say, "It's beyond me," and he, too, left.

Just then the bull took a new fit of struggling and I heard the loud buzz of a rattlesnake behind me. I almost dropped my holt on the bull's tail then, but I had acquired the .habit of holding on to it by this time, so glanced over my shoulder to see how far the snake was from me. I discovered he was only about ten feet behind me, coiled up and mad about something. He was about four and a half feet long and big around as my wrist, and didn't seem to have any notion of going around, but just laid there coiled up, and every time the bull or me moved, would begin to rattle and draw his head back and forth, run out his tongue and act disagreeable. Several times he started to uncoil and crawl in my direction, but I stirred up the bull to floundering around and bluffed the snake out of coming any closer. Still he seemed to like our company, and finaly went to sleep; but every time I and the bull got to threshing around, he would drowsily sound his rattle, as much as to say, "I am still

here; don't crowd me any." It was now about two
o'clock in the afternoon. I felt a kind of a goneness
in my stomach, but my thirst was something awful,
and in my mind's eye I could see the boys in town
setting in the card-room of the saloon around the
poker tables behind stacks of red, white and blue
chips, drinking Scotch highballs, while I was out on
that high mesa dying of thirst and holding down a
little black bull maverick with nothing for company
but that old fat rattlesnake who insisted on staying
there to see how the bull and I come out.

I hoped against hope that when old Billy arrived
at the ranch some one would start back with him to
hunt me up, but I remembered that most everybody
at the ranch had gone up in the mountains trout fishing and wouldn't be back till night, and then I wondered which would live the longest, me or the bull,
and I thought about slipping away from him while
he was quiet; but the moment I would loosen up on
his tail he would commence threshing around trying
to get up, still I kept fooling with him. I'd loosen up
on his tail, and then when he tried to get up, throw
him back; so pretty soon he didn't pay any attention
when I loosened up, and I thought I would try a sneak.

However, in order to make him think I still had hold of his tail, I tied the end of it into a hard knot.

I looked around for his snakeship, as I had got to sneak back towards him, but he was sound asleep, and as the bull was pretty quiet, I sized up the country back of me and spied a gulch with steep broken banks about one hundred and fifty yards away, and made up my mind that that was the place to get to. So slipping by the snake I made the star run of my life for that gulch.

I had run about fifty feet when that bull first realized some of his company was missing, and jumping to his feet looked around and caught sight of me, and giving a snuff that I can hear in my dreams to this day, he was after me. Talk about running. I remember a jackrabbit jumped up in front of me, but I hollered to him to get out of the way. The bull caught up before I quite got to the gulch, but hesitated for a moment where to put his horns, and sort a-throwed his head up and down for a time or two, like he was practicing—kind a-getting a swing like throwing a hammer. When he got his neck to working good, biff! he took me and I went sailing through the air, but when I come down it was on the bank of the gulch, and before he could pick me up again I was over and under that bank. It was about fifteen feet to the bottom and straight up and down, but there was a little shelf of hard dirt on the side, and I caught on there and was safe. He had gone clear over me into the gulch, but was up and bawling and jawing around in a minute. However, he couldn't get up to me, so looked around, found a trail leading out of the gulch, and went up on top, then come around and looked down at me. He was mad clear through; went and hunted up the old rattlesnake, and after pawing and bellowing around him, charged him and got bit on the nose. Then he saw my Stetson hat, and giving a roar, went after it, and putting his horn through it, went off across the hills mad clear through, full of snake poison, with my Stetson hat on one horn, and that was the last I saw of the little black bull.

CHAPTER XVII.

Stealing Crazy Head's War Ponies.

We all got to talking about looking over your shoulder, and the boys asked me if I had ever had to look over my shoulder, and I related to them the following incident in my career on the plains:

In the year 1880-81 the first cattle herds were driven to northern Wyoming and turned loose along Tongue River, Powder River and the Little Horn, and while the Injuns in southern Montana at that time were not very hostile, yet they kept stealing our hosses and butchering the cattlemen's cattle and committing all kinds of petty crimes, and once in a while when they found a white man riding alone in the hills didn't scruple to murder him. But stealing hosses was their long suit. Now, I only had four hosses at that time, and was working out by the month for a cow outfit at $50 a month and board. I thought everything of these four hosses, as they was the sum total of my possessions except about $500 I had due me in wages. And when these hosses was missing one day and a hunter reported seeing a band of Injuns prowling around, I was pretty well worked up. A good many of the settlers in northern Wyoming at that time had had their hosses stolen by the Injuns, but when they found them in the Injuns' possession were unable to get them, as the Injuns refused to give them up and would drive the white men out of their camp. I had always made a loud talk when these men related their experiences, that if ever any Injuns stole my hosses and I found them in their possession I'd take them hosses and no Injun would drive me a step in any direction. So when a freighter reported seeing some Injuns on the Little Horn River, going north with my hosses, the cowboys all said now was the time for me to make good all my loud talk about taking my hosses away from the Injuns if they stole them.

I had considerable trouble to get anyone to go with me, but finally persuaded a boy by the name of King, who was about 17 years old at the time, and getting three hosses from the outfit I worked for, which was the PK cattle outfit, we packed one of the hosses with bed and grub, and riding the other two we struck out north down the Little Horn River. After traveling along the river for several days we crossed and went over on the Big Horn River, and keeping up this river to the Big Horn Mountains, came across about two hundred Injuns camped at the base of the mountains. As soon as we got in sight of their cayuses we saw two of my hosses running with theirs. When we rode into their camp they appeared friendly enough till they found out we wanted these two hosses. I could talk the Injun language, and after making one of the petty chiefs of their band a few little presents, King and I went out to catch our two hosses, but they had been running with the Injuns' cayuses so long we couldn't get near them. Finally we tried to drive them away from the Injuns' cayuses, but about twenty Injuns had come up to us and told us to let the hosses alone and go away. They had their guns, and while they didn't point their guns at me, they kept sticking them against King's breast and threatening to shoot if he didn't go at once. I now offered to pay them if they would catch the two hosses. Every Injun wanted from four to twenty dollars apiece. As there were about twenty Injuns it amounted to about $300. The Injuns rounded up all their cayuses, and getting them in a safe corral, caught my two hosses.

I now instructed King to take the saddle off the hoss he was riding and tie the hoss to the pack-hoss, and I also done this with the one I was riding. We then turned them loose and the three animals immediately started south towards Wyoming. I then told King to saddle one of the hosses that the Injuns had caught for us, but pay no attention to the Injun who was holding it. I saddled the other animal; two Injuns each had a rope on the hoss's neck. When we got them saddled and bridled, I told King to get on his, and I got on mine. The Injuns were standing all around us as well as the squaws and papooses, but they had all laid down their guns. I pulled my Winchester out of the saddle scabbard and throwing a shell in the barrel, I told King to pull his sixshooter and cut the Injun's rope that was on his hoss's neck. He said: "The Injuns will shoot me if I do." I said: "I will shoot you right now if you don't." Although he was very much excited, he managed to pull his knife out of his belt and cut the Injun's rope, and immediately started off after the pack-hoss and saddle hosses on a dead run. The Injuns all set up a howl, and the squaws began bringing the guns out of the teepees. But I kept throwing my Winchester down on first one and then another. The Injuns kept up an awful din hollering to one another, all the squaws yelling to kill the masacheta (white man). But I could hear the chief's voice above them all, telling them not to shoot me. The two Injuns holding the hoss having dropped their ropes, I suddenly threw the ropes off my hoss's neck and reaching down grabbed a papoose, five or six years old, and throwing it up in the saddle with me, galloped away. I knew they wouldn't shoot at me as long as I held to that papoose. But it was like holding on to a full-grown wildcat. I was carrying my Winchester in one hand, guiding my hoss with the same hand and trying to hold on to that little biting, scratching, hair-pulling, shrieking papoose with the other. My hoss was bounding over rocks and sage brush. But he was a magnificent animal and in less time than it takes to tell I was out of gunshot, and then I dropped that shrieking little Injun devil on a sage bush and galloped off in the gathering darkness.

I soon caught up with King. We traveled all night and the next day. Putting him on the trail to Wyoming with all the hosses but the one I was riding, I turned north again to find the other two hosses. That day I met a Piegan Injun that I was acquainted with, and he told me old Crazy Head's band was camped on the Yellowstone River, and that they had my other two hosses and tried to sell them to him.

I rode into Fort Custer and told my story to Jim Dunleavy, the post scout and interpreter, and wanted him to introduce me to the post commander and get me a permit to be on the reservation. But the post commander refused to see me and sent word for me to get off the reservation, or he would put me in the' guard house. But I struck out through the hills north, and that afternoon came in sight of Crazy Head's camp. I found an Injun boy herding a large bunch of cayuses about a mile from camp, with my two hosses in the bunch. I rode into the herd and had my hosses roped and tied together before the Injun had recovered from his surprise, and started back south.

But now a new idea took possession of me. Why not steal some Indian cayuses and get even? There was a stage line running through the reservation them days, and I knew the stock tender at the stage ranch, fifteen miles from Fort Custer, at the Fort

Custer battle-ground. So waiting till dark I went there, and getting something to eat and leaving the two hosses, I started back to Crazy Head's camp. It was a bright, moonlight night and I found the Injuns' cayuses grazing in the same place. Looking around cautiously I discovered two fine-looking, coal black cayuses grazing by themselves about two hundred yards from the main bunch. Slipping up close to them I threw my rawhide rope over one of them, and, as he was perfecty gentle, started to lead him to a little patch of timber, intending to hobble him and come back and get his mate. But as soon as I started to lead him off, his mate followed him, so I just kept going till I got to the stage station, twenty miles from there, about 3 o'clock in the morning. Getting a bite to eat from the old stock tender and showing him the two cayuses I had stole, he told me he knew the cayuses and that they were old Crazy Head's war ponies.

I had been in the saddle now for twenty-four hours without any rest, but dare not stop a moment, for I knew the Injuns and troops both would be after me as soon as Crazy Head missed his ponies. So necking the two to my other two hosses I started for

9—

Wyoming, ninety miles away. The Little Horn River was very high, swimming a hoss from bank to bank, and the stage hadn't been able to get through for some time. The recent rains made the ground soft, and I knew the Injuns would have no trouble tracking me. But they wouldn't miss the ponies till 6 o'clock in the morning, so I would have twenty miles the start and certainly three hours of time. But there was the danger of meeting other Injuns who would know Crazy Head's ponies, and I might meet some scouting soldiers and have to give an account of myself, not having any permit. I didn't mind swimming the Little Horn River, if I hadn't the hosses to drive, but it's hard work for a hoss to swim in a swift current where the waves out about the middle are running big and high, as they do in mountain streams, and drive some loose hosses. But I made the hosses all plunge in and started for the other shore, two hundred yards away. They all swam like ducks at first crossing, but I would have to swim the river seven times if I kept the valley, and knew I would lose time if I went through the hills. So I kept on in a tireless lope, mile after mile, and all the time looking back over my shoulder.

"Looking Over My Shoulder."

Now I knew the Injuns couldn't be in twenty miles of me, but nevertheless I kept looking over my shoulder to make sure, and I looked ahead, and every moving bush along the stream looked like a soldier or an Injun, and every jackrabbit that jumped up side the road, every sage hen that flew out the grass and startled my hosses nearly made me jump out of my skin. Everything that moved in the distance looked like old Crazy Head to me. Talk about looking over your shoulder, boys; why, my neck got in the shape of a corkscrew. Then I came to another cross-ing of the river. I never stopped to look at the high rolling black waters, but plunged my hosses in and struck out for the other side. I again made it in safety, and stopping just long enough to tighten my saddle cinches, took another look over my shoulder and hit that lope again and made up my mind I wouldn't be caught. But supposing I was caught, what kind of a story could I tell? And so I tried to figure out a defense for being found with them two black hosses. I couldn't think of anything or any story but what looked fishy and showed I was a thief, and it seemed as if every one else would know it. I remember after I became an officer of the law, several years after this event happened, I caught a poor devil skinning a beef one day that didn't belong to him, and as I rode up on him and told him to turn the beef over so I could see the brand, he dropped his skinning knife and looking up at me with guilt and terror in his face, he says, "You know how it is yourself." And I said, "Yes, Bill, I know how it is. I was a thief once, but the people are paying me now to uphold the law. Besides I stole Injun hosses and you are stealing white men's beef." And then at the memory of my ride on the Little Horn that day I looked over my shoulder again, and when I looked back for Bill he was gone, and somehow I was kind of glad, for I had a fellow feeling for him.

But to return to my story. When I had swum the Little Horn the fourth time I was forty miles on my journey, and while the iron grey Oregon hoss I was riding seemed as fresh as ever, the black Indian ponies seemed to be getting tired. When I struck the next ford on the river I was fifty miles on the way and it was only 9 o'clock. I was feeling pretty good. But this time when we got out about the middle of the river where the waves were high and rolling, one of the Injun ponies stopped swimming and commenced to float down stream with his nose in the water and dragging the one he was necked to with him. I started after them and by a good deal of urging got my hoss alongside, and throwing my rope on them finally towed them ashore. The pony laid in the shallow water at the shore for a long time, and I thought he was dead, but he finally came to and got up. But he was full of water and pretty groggy.

I found the other two, and getting them together again started on, but knew I would have to take to the hills now when I came to the river again, which I did, and hadn't rode over five miles in the hills skirting the river till, coming up on a high divide and looking down in the valley of the river, I saw a camp of five or six hundred Injuns; but they didn't see me, and I kept on till I came to Owl Creek, which empties into the Little Horn, and it was bank full of cream-colored, muddy water. The banks were steep and I couldn't guess at the depth of the water, which was of the consistency of gumbo soup. However, I drove the hosses into it, first having untied them from one another, as the buffalo trail going down into it was very narrow. As each hoss plunged in he went completely out of sight, and I couldn't guess how far he went under water. But they all clambered up on the other bank, and I see I had got to follow them, so plunged in. As my hoss jumped off that high bank, I grabbed my nose and under that yellow water we went. It seemed like we never would find the bottom, but finally did, and came back to the surface and scrambled up the bank. My fine buckskin shirt and leggings made but a sorry appearance. My six-shooter and holster were full of yellow mud the same as my Winchester, and it took me an hour to clean my guns and get that yellow mud off my hat and clothes. But I had no more streams to cross, except Tongue River, which is in Wyoming, and I crossed it a little after dark and got to my own ranch at 9 o'clock that evening, having ridden the same hoss one hundred and six miles since 3 o'clock that morning.

That grey hoss is still living and is 30 years old now, and is well known by all the old-timers in northern Wyoming. I laid down and slept for twenty hours, and when I reported at the roundup with my four hosses and the two Injun ponies besides, I got a hearty handshake all around. The boys made up a pot of a hundred dollars and gave it to me for the Injun ponies, and then played a game of freeze-out to see who should have them.

I've never had the least inclination to look over my shoulder since.

CHAPTER XVIII.

The Cattle Queen's Ghost.

When darkness overshadows a lone cow ranch, wild and drear,
One's nerves they get a-trembling in a way that seems so queer;
When you *feel* the spirits round you, 'tis idle then to boast
You don't believe those stories you've heard about the ghosts.

One dark, rainy evening while we were waiting on a sidetrack the boys insisted I should tell them some adventure of mine. So after considerable urging I told them an actual experience I had, that has always convinced me that murdered people's ghosts come back and haunt the place they were murdered in.

Twenty years ago Jerry Wilson was known as the cattle king of the Platte River. His cattle roamed for hundreds of miles up and down the main river and all its tributaries, and, as the cowboys used to say, no one man could count them even if they was strung out, cause he couldn't count high enough.

Jerry had a beautiful wife and two lovely children, a boy and a girl, and for years he and his family had no settled place to live, but went around amongst his different ranches, staying awhile at each one, the children being kept in school in Chicago, except in the summer time when they came West to stay on some cattle ranch with their parents. Finally Jerry Wilson bought a new ranch up in the south part of South Dakota, on Battle Creek, and stocking it up with registered cattle and fine horses, built a fine house, furnished it very expensively and settled on this ranch for their home. He built magnificent barns that were the talk of the whole country, and spent a small fortune in building up and beautifying this ranch. But one day Jerry was riding his horse after a cow on a hard run. The horse stepped in a badger hole and fell on top of him, crushing in his ribs and otherwise injuring him so he only lived long enough to be carried to the house and bid his wife and children goodbye before he died.

Mrs. Wilson mourned for Jerry a long time, but the care of her two children and the increasing cattle herds occupied her mind and time to such an extent that her grief had settled into a quiet sadness, when a young man from New York City, who had been discarded from home by his family for his profligate excesses, came to Battle Creek, and stopping at Mrs. Wilson's ranch was (as is the custom at all cattle ranches in the West) made welcome to stay as long as he wanted to. At this time Jerry Wilson had been dead seven years. His daughter, who was the oldest of the two children, had married a prominent lawyer of Chicago. The son was in school in the same city, and Mrs. Wilson made her home at the Battle Creek ranch. She had successfully carried on all her cattle enterprises and was known all over the West as the Cattle Queen. She was about 40 years old at this time, still a beautiful woman and had received many offers of marriage, but had rejected them all till this graceless and unprincipled scoundrel from New York, whose name was Clayton Allen, came to the ranch. Mrs. Wilson had arrived at the age where a great many women begin to hanker for a young man's society and attention, and was soon violently in love with Clayton Allen; and he, seeing a chance to get hold of large sums of money to gamble and go on sprees with, and knowing he could never hope to get any more from his family, laid siege to the Cattle Queen's heart and herds with all the wiles he was capable of.

To make the story short, Mrs. Wilson married this worse than scamp and learned too late to regret her mistake. He persuaded her first to sell all her great cattle herds and ranches and invest all the money in bonds, which she did, keeping only the ranch and blooded cattle on Battle Creek. He now persuaded her to go to New York City with him, and soon as they arrived he joined his old gang of profligates and spent his nights with gay men and women, only coming to see her when his money was exhausted, and then only long enough to get more money. In vain she plead with him. Finally, in sorrow and grief, not having seen him for several days, she took the train for the West and returned alone to her old Battle Creek home.

She had been home about a month, staying in her room alone most of the time, weeping and crying, when one stormy, black night Clayton Allen returned about 10 o'clock. He immediately went to his wife's rooms. The servants heard loud talking and angry words between them for some time, and apparently he was demanding money and she was refusing to give him any. There was a large hall that ran through the center of the house, dividing the building its entire length. The servants had their rooms and the dining-room was on the west side of this hall, and the Cattle Queen had her parlors and sleeping apartments on the other side. About 11 o'clock the servants heard their mistress walking up and down this hall, crying and moaning, but on opening their door that led into the hall found she had gone back into her rooms, but Clayton Allen came in the hall just then and asked the housekeeper to bring a bottle of wine, as her mistress was ill and wanted some. The wine was brought, and Clayton Allen taking it out of her hand at the door closed the door in her face, telling her if she was wanted he would call her. Thirty minutes later the housekeeper heard her mistress scream for help in the hall, and rushing in found her lying on the floor in violent spasms, and picking her up carried her to the bed, only to see her die the next moment. The death-stricken woman only spoke once as she was being carried to the bed. She whispered in the housekeeper's ear, "Mr. Allen has poisoned me."

All of the Cattle Queen's money and bonds were kept in a portable safe and where she kept the keys hidden no one knew. But at the funeral the lawyer from Chicago, who, it will be remembered, married Jerry Wilson's daughter, appeared on the scene, and after a consulation with the housekeeper and cowboys at the ranch, Clayton Allen disappeared, in fact the cowboys kidnapped him and kept him guarded in an old dugout for several days, and when they let him go the lawyer had returned to Chicago. The safe disappeared at the same time the lawyer left. So Clayton Allen never got the enormous fortune that was in the safe, but he got an administrator appointed, and the administrator sold the herd of fine cattle at the Battle Creek ranch to me, as also the use of the ranch for one year, and the hay.

I tried to get some cowboys living in that part of the country to take care of the ranch and cattle, but all of them promptly refused, saying they wouldn't stay there for any amount of money. Then I sent some of my men from my Wyoming ranch, where I was living at the time, but in a week they came back, looking shamefaced and sulky, but refusing to stay at the Battle Creek ranch. After I questioned them pretty sharply, they said they didn't believe much in ghosts, but the Cattle Queen's ghost was too much for them. They said from 10:30 o'clock in the evening till after midnight she tramped up and down the hall in the house, crying, screaming and groaning. They said the doors leading from the hall to the Cattle Queen's rooms kept opening and shutting, and they could hear her talking and expostulating with someone and walking back and forth from the hall to her rooms. I had an old man working for me at the time who was almost totally deaf, so I sent him and my own son, Georgie, who was a manly, brave little fellow of 12 years, to the ranch. I had a talk with George before they started and told him all about it. I said some one was trying to buy the ranch cheap and was making these disturbances in order to give the ranch the name of being haunted. But in a week I got a letter from my boy, saying there might not be any such things as ghosts, but there was certainly some kind of carrying on in the hall of that old house every night, and wanting me to come up. So taking my gun and dog, I went up there to lay the ghost. My dog was one of the largest specimens of the big blue Dane breed and wasn't afraid of anything. And I said to myself, "Now I will nail these parties and convince my son while he is young that there isn't any such things as ghosts."

When I arrived at the ranch I found Deaf Bill, as we called him, and my little boy had taken up their quarters in the housekeeper's room, which was in the extreme western portion of the house, which was built without any upstairs, all the rooms being on the ground floor. I went into the hall of the house and found that the doors at each end of the hall were locked from the inside, the keys being in the locks. I next went into the parlors and sleeping apartment used by the Cattle Queen in her lifetime and where she met her tragic death, and found the curtains all down and the windows closed with catch locks and screens outside of the windows. Everything was apparently in the same condition as when the rooms were fastened up after her death. Her books, and pictures, and paintings, and wardrobe, and easy chairs were all there, just as if she might have stepped out expecting to be back at any moment.

I raised a window in her bedroom with some difficulty, as I wanted to air the room a little, for I had made up my mind to sleep in that bed that night in those haunted rooms and convince superstitious people that I at least wasn't afraid of ghosts. I tried to get my little boy to sleep in there with me, but with pale cheeks and staring eyes and chattering teeth he begged so hard that I didn't insist on it. I have al-

10—

ways been thankful that I didn't oblige him to stay with me that dreadful night.

When I retired, about 8:30 that evening, with my dog and gun into the haunted rooms I was very tired from my long drive from the railroad, and setting the lamp on a stand at the head of the bed and putting my six-shooter under my pillow I called my dog to the side of the bed and laying down with my clothes on, pulled some blankets over me, blew out the light and immediately went to sleep.

How long I slept I know not, but was awakened by my dog who was whining and licking my face. When I first woke up I didn't remember for a moment where I was, but the next moment heard a long-drawn sigh across the room from me and could hear somebody walking on the carpet. I bounded up and had just lit the lamp when I heard someone open the door from the parlor into the hall, and the next moment heard an agonizing cry for help in the hall. I now grabbed the lamp and my six-shooter and running through the two parlors opened the hall door suddenly, just after hearing the second cry for help, and found that the hall was absolutely empty, the doors at each end still being locked, and the door that

The Cattle Queen's Ghost.

led into the servants' part of the house was also locked from my side of the hall, as I had locked it when I went through to go to bed.

I went back into the two parlors and sleeping apartments and searched them thoroughly, even the wardrobes and clothes closets; tried all the windows, but there was no trace of any living person's presence. I then noticed my dog. He had crawled under the bed and was lying there whining in the most abject terror. I dragged him out and kicked him a couple of times and told him to "watch them." But apparently he'd had all the ghost business he cared about, for he lay at my feet trembling and whining. Disgusted with him, I laid down again, thinking I would blow out the light, but be ready with my six-shooter and some matches and catch whoever it was prowling around that house, trying to hoodoo the place.

I hadn't any more than laid down and blown out the light before my dog was trying to get out of the window back of my bed and whining piteously, and then I heard a woman crying in the same room with me and coming slowly towards my bed. I began to get nervous, but scratched a match and in the flickering light saw that the room was absolutely empty. But as the match went out I heard someone run through the parlor, open and shut the door into the hall, and then heard a long despairing cry for help in a woman's voice. I plucked up the little courage I had left, ran to the hall door, opened it, and, lighting a match, gazed up and down that empty hall, seeing nothing or nobody. But as the match flickered and went out there came a breath of cold air right in my face, and then out of that black darkness, seemingly right at my shoulder, arose that awful blood-curdling cry for help again, and as my blood froze in my veins my dog answered the cry with one of those long, despairing, drawn-out, mournful howls that dogs always give as a premonition of death in the family. I tottered back to the bed and vainly tried to light a match, but was too nervous; then hearing that light footstep and that rustling presence coming from the hall through the parlors again towards the bed, I dropped the match and pulling a lot of blankets and bed covers over my head, I huddled down in a heap and lay there trembling with fright and horror till the next morning, when I heard my boy pounding on the outside of the window and calling me to breakfast.

No money would have induced me to have stayed another night on that ranch, and getting an offer next day for the cattle, I sold them. Five years afterwards I saw a man who had come by the Cattle Queen's ranch and he said nobody lived there. The house and barns were all out of repair; the fields overgrown with weeds and an air of desolation to the whole premises. The administrator had finally sold the property for a song to an easterner and he moved his family up there in the day time. He had to go back to town that night for another load of his goods, and when he returned to the ranch the next day, he found his wife roaming around the fields a raving maniac, and she is still in the asylum in South Dakota. They say the Cattle Queen's ghost still keeps éntire possession, and will till her murderer is punished for his crimes.

CHAPTER XIX.

PACKSADDLE JACK'S DEATH.

Packsaddle Jack had got tired of filing off wrinkles one night, and, not being sleepy, walked on ahead of the special till he came to a sidetrack. Lying down there on the embankment he went to sleep and caught a violent cold, from which he never recovered. It settled into a bad cough, and the wrinkle dust seemed to aggravate it. Still he insisted on taking his regular shift in spite of our remonstrances, and the harder he coughed the harder he'd file. As the motion of filing and coughing is almost the same, he seemed to make better time coughing when he was filing, and vice versa, but finally he became so weak that he couldn't leave the way-car any more, and we knew it would be a question of a very few days till old Packsaddle would be swimming his bronk across the River Styx. He became very quiet and thoughtful those days—seemed to do a heap of studying—and one bright, sunny afternoon he called me over to his corner of the way-car and told me he had a dream the night before and it made such an impression on him he wanted to tell it to me.

He said in the start of his dream he seemed to be there on the way-car planning how much he could possibly get out of what cattle was left when he got to Omaha, when it seemed all of a sudden there was a mighty well-dressed cowpuncher riding a big paint hoss and leading another all saddled and bridled came right up to him and says: "Packsaddle, come with me." He said the stranger had on a big Stetson hat, a mighty nice embroidered blue shirt, with red silk necktie and white fur shaps, high-heeled boots, and a pearl-handled .45 six-shooter. He was riding Frazier's famous Pueblo saddle, had a split-eared bridle and was rigged out every way that was proper. Said he asked the stranger where he wanted him to go, and the stranger told him they was going to a country where there was no sheep or sheepmen; where the grass grew every year; where the cattle was always fat; where they drove their cattle to market place of shipping them; where hard winters, horn flies, heel flies and mange was unknown. He said the stranger made such a square talk he finally made up his mind to go with him, although he had some doubts, not knowing the fellar. So getting on the led hoss, he was kind of surprised to find the stirrups just his length and the saddle just fitted him.

He said they started off kind a slow at first, in a little jog trot, but directly got to loping, and finally, after crossing a lot of mean-looking country, they came to a big river and his guide told him they had got to swim their horses across it as there was no bridge. The stranger said lots of smart men had tried to build a bridge across this river, and some people had deluded themselves into thinking they knew of a bridge that they could get across on, but always when it came to crossing they couldn't exactly locate their bridge and had to plunge in with the crowd. Packsaddle said it was a mighty ugly-looking stream. It was wide and deep and looked like it was rising. The water was black as ink and the waves out toward the middle was rolling mountain high. Still there appeared to be people all along the shore, a-plunging in and starting for the other side. There was a large crowd scattered along and most of them didn't seem to see the river till they fell off backwards into it.

They would be laughing and cutting up, with their backs to the river and all of a sudden get too close; a little piece of bank would crumble off, and with a despairing cry they disappeared beneath the black waters and was seen no more. Some apparently mighty rich people dashed up with carriages and servants, and taking a sack of gold in each hand would offer that to the river, thinking probably they wouldn't have to cross if they offered it some gold. But of all the people who came to the river, only a very few ever turned back, although most of them seemed to want to. He noticed a few that looked like farmers' wives who came up, and soon as they saw the river a smile of content came on their faces and they slid into the boiling water as naturally as though it was wash-day. There was a class of men, too, who came up with a determined look on their countenances, and without the slightest hesitation plunged into the awful stream and struck out for the other side. These men all had cowboy hats on, and when Packsaddle asked his guide who they were, he said they were cowmen who had been shipping their cattle to the Omaha market, and their cattle had starved to death on the stock-yard transfer waiting to be unloaded.

Some there was that looked like pettifogging lawyers and cheap politicians, who, when they arrived at the river, flourished a handful of annual passes over different lines, looking for a pass over the river, but not getting it, turned back and wouldn't cross, and the guide told Packsaddle that he guessed this class of people never did cross, as they seemed to get thicker every year.

Packsaddle said at first he kind of hated to cross the river, as his guide said none ever returned, and he couldn't see the other bank very plainly, and was in some doubt as to what kind of a country was on the other side, although there was hundreds of big, fat, red-faced looking men, dressed in black, standing along the shore where he was, telling everybody what kind of a country was on the other side. They differed a great deal in their description of it, but that was probably on account of what different people wanted. All these black-robed, fat-looking rascals got money out of the crowds and seemed to be doing a thriving business by fixing up people to cross and giving them encouragement. Most all of them was selling some kind of a patented life-preserver to wear across the river, and each one shouted out the merits of his life-preserver till their noise drowned the roar of the river, and they tried to get lots of people to cross the river that hadn't got anywhere near the bank, just to sell them a life-preserver.

Packsaddle had noticed all these things as they waited on the bank a moment, and then, he said, they plunged their hosses in and started swimming for the other side. The other bank, he said, was sorter obscured by a mist or fog, and he didn't see it till most there, but saw worlds of all kinds of people struggling in the black water of the river. Packsaddle said his hoss swam high in the water, never wetting the seat of his saddle, and he felt just like he was getting home from the general roundup. When they struck the bank there was a bunch of cowboys helped his hoss up the bank, gave him a hearty handshake all around and made him welcome every way. When he turned around to thank his guide that gentleman had vanished, and the cowboys told him his guide was a regular escort across the river for cowmen and cowboys; that most everybody had to get across the best way they could, but cowmen and cowboys always had a good hoss to ride and a guide; that one reason for this was that they was most always mighty good to a hoss and thought a heap of them. They said, though, that there was a lot of boats with cushioned seats, and mighty comfortable, that brought over the poor old widder women and farm-. ers' wives and orphan children that had been abused and starved till they just had to cross the river to get away.

Packsaddle said it looked like a mighty good country, lots of fat cattle, the finest hosses he ever see, lots of cowboys laying under the mess-wagon bucking monte and everybody winning, while the roundup cooks had pots and bakeovens steaming with roast veal, baking powder biscuits and cherry roll. He said the boss of one of these outfits hired him on the spot, and giving him a string of fat hosses to ride, he picked out a black pinto with watch eyes and saddled him. Soon as he got on this hoss it started to buck and he said he dreamed that hoss throwed him so high that he saw he was coming down on the other side of the river and it disgusted him so he woke up.

Packsaddle was very weak when he got through telling his dream, and after taking a drink of water he told me he thought we was all making a mistake trying to make money raising cattle. He'd heard

Packsaddle Jack.

about some place in the East where they just issued stock, place of raising it, and that certainly must be the place to go. He'd heard of two or three men, probably stockmen, who get together in New York City, issued just millions of stock in one day, and he was satisfied that was one thing made our stock so cheap. For himself, he said, he liked that country he saw in his dream and thought he'd go there pretty soon.

While we were talking the head brakeman came in and said there was a cow dead in the car next the engine. Packsaddle gave a gasp or two, and when I bent down over him he whispered he would go and round her up; and when I looked at him again he was dead.

Poor old Packsaddle! His early life had been embittered by the discovery that a married woman (whom he was in the habit of visiting in the absence of her husband down in Texas where he was raised) was untrue to him, and on meeting his rival at the lady's house when her husband had gone to mill with a grist of corn, he promptly filled his rival's anatomy full of lead and came away in such a hurry that he had to borrow a jack-mule and packsaddle from a man

11—

that was prospecting, and. rode this packsaddle to Wyoming, and thus acquired the euphonious name of Packsaddle Jack. Although he was cheerful at times, yet the memory of this woman's perfidy to him cast a gloom of melancholy over his after life which was never entirely dispelled. He never whined when he lost his money bucking monte, always had a good supply of tobacco and cigarette papers of his own and never failed to pass them around. While he didn't have much love for women or Injuns, he loved a good hoss and twice owed his life to his hoss when he had a brush with Cheyenne Injuns in early days in northern Wyoming.

In a burst of confidence a few days before his death he told me he had endured the worst kind of hardships all his life. Winter and summer he had lived on the plains and in the mountains without shelter, by open campfires, lots of times without much to eat; had been hunted and shot at for days and nights by Cheyenne Injuns and never met with the privations and discomforts he had on this trip. And as for slowness, he said he hired out one time in Texas when he was a boy, to help drive 900 tame ducks across the swamps of Louisiana to New Orleans to market; said the trail was so narrow that only one duck at a time could walk in it and sometimes no trail at all, just high grass and swamp brush, and yet they beat the time of a cattle special away yonder.

THE SPIRIT OF PACKSADDLE FOLLOWS THE DEAD COW.

———

A stock train was waiting on a sidetrack one day
For gravel trains going some other way;
And as they waited the cattle grew old,
The stockmen grew haggard, the weather turned cold.

Their stomachs were empty, they were starving in fact,
While the stock train was waiting on its lonely sidetrack.
The reports said the markets were lower each day,
While the cattle grew thinner, the stockmen grew grey.

An old, grizzled cattleman spoke up at last,
Said he to the cowboys, "The time it is past,
To make mon out of cattle or get any dough,
This going to market by rail is a little too slow.

The railroad companies' tariffs get higher each year,
Their passes get fewer, till I very much fear
That ahead of our stock train we will have to walk
And wait for the cattle train to get up our stock.

Let us up and be doing and build a big merger trust,
And sell stock to suckers and let them go bust,
And for every steer issue millions of shares,
Let other people worry how to get railroad fares.

We will issue bonds and certificates and thus raise our
  stock;
In place of breeding Shorthorns we will make a swift talk;
Have our shares all printed in red, green and gold,
Sell them in the stock market to the young and the old.

And thus live by our cuteness and work of our brains
In place of starving on special stock trains.
We will have servants and waiters, the best in the land;
Governors and princes will give us the glad hand."

Just then the front brakeman stuck in his head,
Saying in the car next the engine an old cow was dead.
The old cowman gave a gasp and his spirit started to ride
To round up that old cow that in the front car had just
  died.

CHAPTER XX.

A Cowboy Enoch Arden.

Just after leaving North Platte, a train of immigrants on their way from Oregon to Arkansas with mule teams went by us, and we found they had a letter for us from Eatumup Jake, who had returned to Utah long ere this to look after his domestic matters. One of the reasons why he abandoned us was to return and look after the education of the twin boys. However, the main reason was that so many reports had come to us from travelers in wagons and sheepherders trailing sheep east, who had come through our neighborhood in Utah, who said that all our friends had given us up for dead, and Eatumup Jake's wife, after putting on mourning for a proper season, had begun to receive the attentions of a widower, who was part Gentile bishop and part Mormon elder.

As Jake was in a hurry when he started back home, he bought him a cheap mustang in place of ac-

164

cepting the transportation which was urged on him by all the principal officers of the railroad. He wrote us that when he arrived on his ranch, his wife was out in the hayfield putting up the third crop of alfalfa. She was driving a bull rake, hauling it into the stack, while one of the twins was driving the mower and the other twin was doing the stacking. The half-breed Mormon-Gentile bishop was standing round with a cotton umbrella over his head, giving orders. Jake's wife didn't know him at first, he had changed so, but the bishop tumbled to him at once and started to leave. However, Jake overtook him and persuaded the bishop to turn aside into a little patch of timber with him, and Jake getting the loan of the umbrella in the painful interview that followed, he left most of the steel ribs of the umbrella sticking in the anatomy of the bishop, and then let the house dog, with the help of the twin boys armed with their pitchforks, assist the bishop clear off the ranch. This was so much better than the old style of Enoch Arden business that Dillbery Ike made up a little rhyme about it after we got Jake's letter, and here it is:

In Utah a cattleman got married in the glow of summer time,
Married a buxom Mormon girl, warm heart and manner kind.
And as the autumnal sun began to tinge things red,
He rounded up his catlte herd and to his bride he said:
"Come hither, dear, and kiss me and sit upon my lap,
For I am going a lengthy journey with my cows and steers
    that 's fat.
I 'm going on the Overland with a special, long stock train."
His bride, she wept and trembled and said, "I 'll ne'er see you
    again.
O Jake, my darling husband, give up this wrong design,
If you must go east with cattle, then try some other line,
For I have heard the stockmen talking and this is what they
    say,
That if you drive your stock to market, that then there 's no
    delay.
But if you get a special train, the railroad has a knack
Of letting you do your running when your train is on a side-
    track.
Some stockmen they have starved to death, and others grow so
    old
That none knew them on their return, so frequent I 've been
    told."
But Jake was young and hearty and his mind was full of zeal
To load his beef on a special and eastward take a spiel.
So he started with his steers and cows in the golden autumn
    time.
Some neighbors also loaded theirs; the cattle were fat and fine.
But they run the stock on the Overland, so slow and awful bum
That stockmen get old and care-worn, staying with a special
    run.
Their wives get weary waiting for hubby's coming home
And flirt with the nearest preacher who drops in when they 're
    alone.

Jake's wife was no exception, and, as time went by, she said,
"If Jake was alive I know he'd come back; he surely must be
    dead."
The good woman put on mourning and mourned for quite a
    time,
But when thus she'd done her duty, she suddenly ceased to
    pine,
And when a Gentile-Mormon preacher dropped in one night to
    tea
She put on her new dress of gingham and was chipper as she
    could be;
Had him eating her pies and jellies that she knew how to make,
Had him sit in the easy rocker, without ever a thought of Jake.
And when the twins got drowsy, she packed them off to bed,
Sat and played checkers with the bishop, just as though poor
    Jake was dead.
When she jumped in the preacher's king row, and had eight
    men to his five, ·
She cared not (she was so excited) whether Jake was dead or
    alive.
But at four o'clock next morning, she roused from sleep with
    a scream;
She'd seen Jake pushing behind a stock train in this early
    morning dream.
And that evening when the lusty preacher came hanging
    around again,
He got but a scanty welcome, for she thought of the special
    train.
For a time she was silent and thoughtful, the dream an im-
    pression had made,
She could still see Jake pushing the special, as it slowly
    climbed the grade.
Now we know how the brave-hearted Jake with the stock train
    had to stay,

How he camped by her side night times as on a sidetrack she
lay.

We know how he pushed so manfully whene'er she climbed a
hill,

In fact every one pushed, even the sheepmen, Cottswool and
Rambolet Bill;

How hunger and famine o'ertook them as slowly they crawled
along,

Their hearts almost broke with home-longing when Jackdo
sung a home song.

Eyes filled with tears that were unbidden, hearts o'erflowing
with pain—

No pen can paint their sorrow as they stayed with this special
stock train.

The passing of poor old Chuckwagon, who slowly starved to
death,

On account of the smell of the sheepmen, he couldn't get his
breath;

Their camping ahead of the special after they had buried
Chuck,

The washing away of the sheepmen, who surely were out of
luck.

They lived in snow huts on the mountain that's known as Sher
man Hill,

Where the last was seen of the sheepmen, Cottswool and Rambolet Bill;

Their arrival at the Windy City that's known as the dead
Shyann,

Some things about Burt and Warren and mayhap another man.

And now with their party diminished by old age, privation and
death,

They still kept plodding on eastward, what of the party was
left.

Till Jake talking with wandering sheepmen, who had trailed
by his cabin home,

Heard of the scandalous preacher, who came when his wife
    was alone;
.Heard of the nightly playing of checkers when the twins were
    safely in bed,
About his wife all the neighbors were talking, her claiming
    that Jake was dead.
Finally through very home-sickness, he started to take the
    back track,
And because he was in such a hurry, he rode all the way horse-
    back.
Arriving in sight of his meadows, a-waving fresh and green,
The alfalfa growing the highest that Jake had ever seen;
Two redheaded boys the hay were pitching; their mother was
    hauling it in.
There was only one blot on the landscape that made Jake feel
    like sin.
'Twas our Gentile-Mormon bishop in the shade of his old
    umbreller,
With his long-tailed coat and eye glasses, he looked like Foxy
    Quiller.
When Jake got close to the bishop he booted him out the field,
The house dog and twins, with their hayforks, finished making
    the elder spiel.
Then Jake gathered his family around him, work was laid by
    for the day,
They told all their joys and their sorrows, so I 've finished my
    lay.

Moral.

The old-fashioned Enoch Arden story was a tale well told;
I can't approach or rival it, nor make a claim so bold.
But the ending of my cowboy Enoch Arden I really like the
    best,
For he fired the interloper out the modern Arden nest.

CHAPTER XXI.

GRAND ISLAND.

Before we arrived at Grand Island we learned from Jackdo that most cowmen unloaded their cattle there and drove them back and forth through the stockyards awhile in order to accumulate a large amount of mud on them. This Grand Island mud is very adhesive and once steers is thoroughly immersed in it the mud sticks to them for weeks and helps very materially in their weight. A shipper told him that before he stopped at Grand Island he used to wonder what cattlemen meant by filling their cattle at Grand Island, but now he knew it was filling their hair full of mud. Sometimes he said the mud was a little too thick, kind of chunky and fell off, and sometimes it had too much water in it and drained off, more or less. But when it was mixed just right it would settle into their hair like concrete cement. It's quite dark in color, fortunately, and if they've had a rain it is easy to get pens where you can im-

170

Joe Kerr Loading Sheep for South St. Joe.

merse your cattle all over and thus make them the color of the Galloways, which is the most fashionable color for cattle in the market.

He said there was cases where cattlemen had got a good fill on Grand Island mud and sold their cattle weighed up there to feeders who put them on full feed for six months and they weighed less in the market than to start with, because the feeders had curried the mud off them. Sometimes he said after people left Grand Island with their cattle and before the mud got well set, there would come a hard rain on them and the mud washed off in streaks and gave the cattle kind of a zebra appearance. Especially was this true where the cattle had originally been white. He said we would be expected to order some hay and pay for it and get the mud for nothing. It was just like a boot-jack saloon, where you bought a high-priced peppermint drop and got a pint of whiskey throwed in.

'Twas here at Grand Island that we met Joe Kerr again. We had met him in Utah before we shipped, and he had tried very hard to get us to ship our cattle to the coming live stock market of the United States at St. Joe. Kerr travels in the interest of the St. Joe stockyards, and while in the fullness of our youth and conceit when we first loaded our stock we wouldn't have taken a suggestion from Teddy Roosevelt, yet we had grown older and had lost some of our self-confidence; in fact, I've often thought since these experiences that the old proverb, "He who ships his range cattle to market place of selling them at home leaves hope behind," would apply to most range shipments.

Now it seems Joe Kerr had kept posted as to our movements right along through friends of his who were in the sheep business and who had trailed their herds past our train at different times on their trip East to sell their sheep for feeders, and Kerr had made such nice calculations by casting horoscopes and looking up the signs of the zodiac that he knew to a month when we would arrive. in Grand Island, and was waiting there to persuade us to ship our stock to St. Joe in place of Omaha. He was right on the spot to help us unload them; knew all the pens where the mud was the deepest, even helped us smear the mud into their hair on the few spots that was missed, when we were swimming them through the mud batter. Joe had loads of sta-

tistics for sheepmen, cattlemen, horsemen and hog-
men that would convince any man that wasn't too
suspicious that St. Joe was the best market. He had
beautiful colored maps of the yards, showing the clear
limpid waters of the Missouri River, flowing along at
the foot of the bluffs; the waters swarming with
steamboats and smaller craft; the city of St. Joe covering the bluffs and river bottoms for miles, and just
down the river at the lower end of this great city was
stockyards and packing plants laid out like some
great city park and hundreds of acres, all paved with
brick, laid into walks and floors for the pens with
perfect precision, and all divided in different com-
partments for all kinds of live stock; everything arranged so sheep could be unloaded one place, hogs another place, cattle another, so as to admit of no delay
in unloading when stock arrived. He told us that
their yards were kept so clean that ladies could walk
all over them in rainy weather without soiling their
costumes. Said no Sheenies were skinning people in
their yards. He made such a square talk we finally
agreed to split the shipment and let part of the train
go to St. Joe, and sent Jackdo along to take care of
the cattle.

12—

CHAPTER XXII.

"SARER."

The rainy season had now set in in good earnest all through Nebraska, and while the natives have typhoid fever and malaria to a more or less extent, yet most of them live through it, but people from the dry mountin regions that have been used to pure air and water all their lives fare worse from these fevers ten times over than the natives, and Dillbery Ike fell a victim right in the start. One evening soon after we left Grand Island I noticed his face was flushed very red, and he complained of a dull headache, but as he had the headache a good deal ever since the railroad police had scalped him at Cheyenne in mistake for a striker, I didn't think so much of his headache. But when I come to look at his tongue and feel his pulse I found every indication of high fever. In a few hours he was out of his mind and talked of shady mountain sides, babbling brooks and clear

176

mountain springs of water, and he talked of his hosses and cattle, his cow ranch and alfalfa meadows, but most of all he talked of "Sarer."

Now Dillbery had only one romance in his life that we knew of, and that happened in this way: Several decades previous to our story the few families living in the vicinity of Dillbery's ranch in Utah had got together and built an adobe school-house, and voting a special tax on the piece of railroad track that run through their part of the country 'had raised enough money to pay for the school-house and hire a school-teacher. At first each of the three married women in the neighborhood wanted to teach the school. Then each of them offered to take turns about teaching it so they could divide the money, but their husbands, who was the directors, wanted a school-marm, so as to have a little young female blood diffused through the atmosphere in that part of the country, and after advertising for a school teacher, the New England brand preferred, got hundreds of answers very shortly. So putting their heads together they selected one that had a kind of crab apple perfume attached to the application, and was worded in such way as to give the reader a notion of pleading blue eyes, with a wealth of golden brown hair and heaving bosom, not too young to teach school nor too old to be romantic and sympathetic, and closed a deal with her to come West and teach their school. She had signed her name Sarah Jessica Virginia Smythe, but was always known as Miss Sarer. When she was about to arrive at the railroad station, thirty miles away, all the married men wanted to go and meet her. All of them had particular business in at the station that day, but none of their wives would stand for it. They said that Dillbery Ike was a bachelor and the proper one to get her.

Now Dillbery Ike was a long, gangling, bashful, backward plainsman, never had a sweetheart and was considered perfectly harmless around women by every one who knew him. The old married men finally agreed to let Dillbery meet the school-marm, but not till each had went through a stormy scene with his wife, in which that good woman had threatened to tear the blanket right in two in the middle with such forcible language that you could almost hear it ripping. Dillbery had got shaved, had his hair cut, put on his best black suit he had bought from a Sheeny, the pants being a trifle of six or eight inche'

The Arrival of Miss "Sarer."

too short for him at the top and bottom both, his coat rather large in the waist, but short at the wrists like the pants, and hitching his mules to his spring wagon, he started bright and early to the station of Kelton, Utah. He arrived about noon, him and his mules white with alkali dust, and finding that the train was twenty-three hours late, stayed at the section house till next day, there being no hotel in Kelton. When the train came along next day about noon, a large, portly lady of uncertain age, with her frizzed-up hair turning grey, her hands full of wraps, lunch baskets, sofa pillows, telescope grips, umbrellers, band-boxes and bird cages, climbed off the train, and the baggageman put off a large horse-hide trunk, from which most of the hair had been worn off, or perhaps scalped off in the troublous times when Washington was crossing the Delaware. When she got this old, bald-headed looking trunk and a couple of shoe boxes with rope handles (that were probably full of Century Magazines) piled up with her other baggage, the newsboy said it looked like an Irish eviction.

When Dillbery saw this old man-hunter and all her luggage, his heart failed him, and he went to the saloon three times to liquor up before he got sand

enough to talk to her. Of course, Dillbery expected
to marry her, no matter what she was like, as the
whole neighborhood where he lived had planned it
ever since the school-marm was talked of, and he
couldn't expect to disappoint the neighbors and still
continue to live there. Still she wasn't exactly what
he had figured in his mind after reading a great many
novels about the rosy-cheeked, small-waisted, dainty-
feet, lily-white hands, wondrous brown hair, blue-
eyed New England darlings, with pretty sailor hats
and tailor-made suits, who come West to teach our
schools and incidentally marry the most expert rop-
ing, best broncho-busting, chief cowpuncher. And
now here was this dropsical-looking old girl, with
fat, pudgy-looking hands and feet like a couple of
poisoned pups, with all this colonial luggage.

However, Dillbery was obliged to take charge of
her and her traps, as he called them, and when he was
finally ready to start, had got everything on the
spring wagon, even to the bird cages, and after getting a final drink with the boys and filling a bottle to
take along, he loaded the old girl in and whipping up
his mules, disappeared in a cloud of alkali dust.

Dillbery sat on his end of the seat, frightened out

of his wits, and Sarah Jessica Virginia Smythe sat on the other end, but, of course, sat on all the vacant seat left by Dillbery, 'cause she couldn't help it, she was built that way, and was even more afraid of Dillbery than he was of her. Although she had always been hunting a man, yet she was in a wild country and a stranger; not a house in sight and night coming on, was with a savage-looking man, who was, undoubtedly, very drunk, and acting very strangely to say the least. As time went on Dillbery got dryer and dryer, and studied a good deal how to get a drink out of his bottle without letting Sarah see him. Finally he concluded he could make some excuse that the load was slipping; he might get around back of the wagon to fix it, and under cover of the darkness quietly get a drink out of his bottle. So when they were crossing a canyon in an unusually lonely spot, he stopped the mules and muttering something about the load, he started to get out, but Sarah thought her hour had come, and throwing her arms (which were like pillow bolsters) around Dillbery's neck, began to scream and piteously beg him not to do her any wrong. The more Dillbery Ike tried to explain, the more Sarah Jessica cried, screamed and sobbed, till finally with a despairing sigh, like unto the collapse of a big balloon, she fainted clear away on his breast, pinning him over the back of the seat, his spinal column slowly but surely being sawed in two over the sharp edge. The horror of poor old Dillbery, when he realized that death from a broken back was only a question of her not coming out of the dead faint, which she seemed to have gotten an allopathic dose of, cannot be described.

When some time had elapsed and she showed no signs of animation, he made a great struggle to get from under her; but it was a vain attempt, he was nailed down as completely as a piece of canvas under a paving block. And when it came over him that he was doomed to this ignominious death, when he fully realized what people would think about him when they found him in this compromising position, and the cowboys would facetiously all agree that he looked like a Texas dogie steer hanging dead on a wire fence after a Wyoming blizzard; when he felt that peculiar, loud buzzing in his ears that is a premonition of death, he made one final desperate struggle, and spitting out a lot of grey hair, hair pins and pieces of switch, which had accumulated in his mouth, he screamed

with all the strength of his lungs in one long despairing cry, the one word "Sarer."

Now in Dillbery Ike's delirium and raging fever
on the stock train, he kept continually giving tongue
in a long, blood-curdling, soul-freezing, despairing cry
to that one word "Sarer." Night and day we had to
listen to that heart-broken cry. Finally, when the
fever was at its highest stage I consulted the conductor of our special about getting a doctor and he
advised me to go back to the last town we had passed
through, where there was a good physician and get
him. He said that we would have plenty of time, as
there was a lonely sidetrack just ahead of the train.
So walking back about ten miles to this town, I secured the services of a doctor, and getting a livery rig
we soon caught up with the special. When the doctor had examined Dillbery's tongue and pulse and had
put his ear to Dillbery's heart while he was giving
one of his despairing cries for "Sarer," he wrote a
prescription in some kind of foreign language which
he interpreted to us, as he said he had written it down
as a mere form to show that he could write in a foreign language. He said our friend was very sick and
the one thing that would save his life was to get

"Sarer" for him. Now, of course, that was an impossibility, but he said all we needed was an imitation "Sarer," something that looked like her and was about her size and form, so after explaining to him what "Sarer" was like, he drove back to town, and when he caught up to us again, brought into the car a wonderful dummy made out of a large sack of bran with a head tied on it composed mainly of a sack of hair, such as plasterers use to mix mortar with. He had a large, but not too large, Mother Hubbard dress on this wonderful dummy, and the whole well perfumed with Florida water. When we laid this imitation "Sarer" in the emaciated arms of poor old Dillbery, his eyes grew moist for a moment, and straining it to his breast he gave a contented sigh or two, whispered "Sarer, Sarer," and dropped off into a healthy slumber, and the doctor said he would live.

Eats Up "Sarer."

Dillbery slept for a long time, and awoke somewhat refreshed, but somewhat under the influence of his animal scalp, and no one being in the car, the spirit of the goat probably overtook him, as he devoured the head of the dummy "Sarer," which will be remembered consisted of plastering hair. Then the spirit of the sheep and the pig coming over him, he devoured the sack of bran, and laying down in front the stove like a Newfoundland dog, he went to sleep. Thus I found him on my return to the car. But, alas! his stomach was too weak to digest all the stuff he had consumed and in a few hours he was in a raging fever and calling for "Sarer" again. But, of course, he had devoured "Sarer," and we had nothing to fix up in the place of the dummy. And while it was heart-rending to hear his sobbing cry for "Sarer" growing weaker and weaker as the night wore on, yet we could only listen and hope. About 4 o'clock in the morning his cries stopped and he seemed to be sleeping for a few minutes, and then opened his eyes and took my hand and in a weak but rational voice told me the story of his boyhood in the following words:

He said he was born in the mountains in Virginia. He was the only child, so far as he knew, of a moonshiner's daughter. His mother was not an unhappy woman, he said, when she had plenty of snuff and moonshine whisky; in fact, was quite gay at times. No one, not even his mother, knew exactly who his father was. Some people said it was a revenue officer and some said it was the member of Congress from that district, but most people thought it was a live stock agent of one of the western railroads. However this may be, he thrived on corn pone, dewberries, wild honey, and sow bosom, and as soon as he got old enough helped his mother cut wood and haul it to town in a two-wheeled hickory cart drawn by a steer. They lived with his grandfather, who was quite a prominent man in that part of Virginia and who was finally killed by revenue officers. His mother was sent to the pen for selling moonshine whiskey and he was taken charge of by a family who immigrated to Utah. He said the last time he saw his darling mother 'twas at their old home in the mountains in Virginia. The steer was hitched to the cart one beautiful spring morning. The sun's rays was just kissing the mountain tops, when two revenue officers had appeared at their home, and after a lively scrap with his mother they had succeeded in arresting her. Not though till she had thoroughly furrowed their cheeks with her finger nails and plenteously helped herself to sundry handfuls of their hair, after which she had peacefully seated herself in the cart and was placidly chewing a snuff stick in each corner of her mouth, when the steer and cart disappeared around a bend in

Dillbery Ike's Darling Mother Under Arrest

the mountain road, and fate had decreed he should never see her again.

The family that took charge of him were neighbor moonshiners and had a day or so after this took place traded off their Virginia estate for a team of antique mules and a linch-pin wagon, and storing a goodly supply of moonshine whiskey, apple jack, corn meal and bacon in the wagon, loaded the family, consisting of nine children, himself included, in the wagon, and immigrated for Utah. He said as long as he was with these people he was treated like one of the family, but as they immigrated back to Virginia the next year they left him in Utah with a poor family and he was hungry many times, and was always telling the children he associated with how big the dewberries grew where he came from, so the other children nicknamed him Dewberry, which was finally changed to Dillbery and that name had stuck to him ever since.

After finishing the story of his boyhood, Dillbery lay quiet for a short time and then motioning me to bend down close to him he whispered to me not to bury him in Nebraska where, he said, the only way a man could hope to be resurrected was in the shape of

13—

a yellow ear of corn, to be fed to a yellow steer, followed by a yellow hog and the hog meat eaten by a yellow-whiskered malarial Populist, and so on. After I promised to see that he was buried on his ranch in Utah, he asked me to sing that old cowboy song, "Oh! give me a home where the buffalo roams, a place where the rattlesnake plays."

THE PASSING OF DILLBERY IKE.

'Twas a dismal night on a way-car, the rain pattering on the
 roof o'erhead,
The man who has told this story was alone with the silent dead.
The voice that had been calling for Sarah was hushed and
 stilled at last,
He had finished telling the story of his childhood's checkered
 past.

No more would he ride the ranges, no more the mavericks
 brand,
Nor subdue the bucking broncho, in that far western land;
Never again to meet the school-marms, when they came trav-
 eling West
Under the guise of school teaching, to get in a bachelor's nest.

Dillberry folded his hands gently, as he quietly went to sleep,
In the death that knows no waking, for which no shipper
 could weep;
While some of his life had been stormy, of hardships he'd had
 his share,
Pen cannot paint a cattleman's troubles, nor picture his heart
 sick care.

When he's got his cattle on a special, and getting a special run,
Death for him hasn't a single terror, he longs for it to come;
And so with poor old Dillbery, when his weary eyes closed in
 death,
Blotted out his sorrows and troubles, all blown away with his
 last breath.

He had gone to meet his grandfather, and get some of his
    latest brew,
For who shall say that old moonshiner had quit distilling some
    mountain dew;
For all say the other world is better, we 'll get what we like
    over there,
While of our joys here we are stinted, in the hereafter we
    get double share.

His eyes grew bright with a vision that he saw on the other
    side,
He got a glimpse of a right good cow country, just before he
    started to ride;
And his eyes lit up with a gladness, his face o'erspread with
    hope,
As without a trace of sadness, his spirit rode away in a lope.

CHAPTER XXIII.

ARRIVAL AT THE TRANSFER TRACK OF SOUTH OMAHA.

One dark, dismal, rainy morning, a little before daylight, I arrived with the remnant of our stock train on the stockyards transfer at South Omaha. The conductor and brakeman ordered me out of the way-car. So picking up my belongings I got out in the mud and rain and looked around for some shelter. There was a lot of railroad tracks and switches, but no houses or hotels, or anyone to inquire from, as I had learnt by experience that conductors, brakemen and switchmen never give any information to stockmen in a dark, rainy night.

So after wandering up and down the tracks for a ways, and not being able to find out which way the town lay I got on top of the stock cars, and huddling down in my rain-soaked rags I prepared to wait till daylight. The rain was very cold, and after a bit turned to snow and chilled me to the bone. But I was afraid to leave the stock cars, as I had never been there before and was sure to get lost if I left the stock, as the town is quite a ways from the transfer. I thought of Dillbery Ike, Packsaddle Jack and old Chuckwagon in the other world, and wondered why I should be left shivering in this' awful storm, suffering the pangs of hunger and cold, while doubtless they had more fire than they really needed. No matter what their condition was in the other world, it was bound to be better than mine. Even the sheepmen's condition in the other world couldn't be much worse, though some claim there is a hell set apart a-purpose for sheepmen on the other side.

My clothes were all worn out long ago; my beard had grown down to my knees and the hair on my head having never been cut since we started, now reached to my waist, and, of course, it and my beard was some protection from the storm. But I realized that if I stayed where I was it would only be a short time till I should meet my comrades who had gone before, and I thought it would be proper to make some preparations for the other world. I never had prayed or went to church much, 'cause a cowman don't have any chance to attend to these, as there is always either some calves to brand Sundays, or else some of the neighbors coming visiting. But I remembered a passage of scripture I had heard when a boy, and it came back to me now and kept ringing in my ears: "Forgive thine enemy." I never had an enemy in my whole life that I knew of, without it was this blamed railroad, and while I wasn't sure they was enemies, yet they had dealt me more misery than anyone, except it might be this stockyards company that was keeping me and my stock out on this transfer, starving and freezing in the storm after me and my steers had all got to be Rip Van Winkles getting that far on the road. I studied over the matter and could see it would be too great a job to forgive them both at the same time, and, of course, couldn't tell how much forgiveness the stockyards company would have to have, as I hadn't got through with them yet. There might be so much against them before they got my cattle unloaded that it would be impossible to forgive it.

It was very lucky, as it turned out afterwards, that I had this forethought, because, as I take it, forgiveness only comes from the heart no matter what your lips say, and your heart is the blamedest thing to control in forgiveness, as well as love, and when that stockyards company finally got around to bring my cattle in and unload them, I reckon it would have been impossible for any mortal man with the least spark of vitality left in his veins to have forgiven them. They have tried over and over to explain it to me by saying that when they built the transfer tracks and unloading chutes, their receipts only run about 1,500 to 2,000 cattle a day, with about the same number of hogs and about 200 sheep. And, now in the fall of the year, their receipts of cattle run up to 7,000 to 12,000 a day, with the same number of hogs and 20,000 to 25,000 of sheep, and they are trying to handle them with the same facilities they had to start with. So they are pretty near always so far behind in unloading stock in the busy season that it takes all the slack business season to finish unloading the stock that accumulated during the rush.

Having made up my mind to put off forgiving the stockyards company till some future date, I turned all my attention to forgiving the railroad company. I had noticed a good many religious people when some one had done them an injury and they couldn't get at them any other way they would pray for them. And while they generally asked the Lord to forgive them,

The Arrival of the Survivor at the Transfer.

yet they always told their side of the story in such a way that if the Lord was anyways easily prejudiced, he would be pretty tolerable slow about handing out any unsought-for clemency to their enemies, as they always started in by telling of all the mean things their enemies had ever done in order to remind the Lord what a big contract it was. After studying the matter over I thought this would be the proper way to pray for the railroad company. But after I got started telling the Lord what mean things they had done, I see 'twas no use to try to finish unless I'd hand the matter down to future generations, as one life wouldn't be long enough to get fairly started in.

THE INFERNO OF THE TRANSFER.

All night long I had heard voices on all sides of me and apparently the owners of them were in the direst distress. Some were praying undoubtedly, but the most were cursing. A few were crying and moaning with the cold and I thought for a long time I must have got into an inferno of lost souls, and added to my sufferings in the storm in which I had come close to death was the terror of listening to these distressing cries, and I longed for daylight to appear so these horrors would be explained.

Daylight began to appear while I was thinking about these things, and I could see other stock trains near me, and on every train I could see one or more miserable wretches like myself huddled down on top of a car in the snow and cold rain, and the only sign of life you could detect was when they took spells of shivering. One of them was pretty close, and I hailed him once or twice, and finally he roused up enough to answer me; but the poor, shivering wretch was so numb with the cold he didn't sense much of anything, and when I asked him why all the shippers stayed out all night with their cattle, place of going into town, he said lots of times cattle were so tired when they got to Omaha and they were so long about getting them to the chutes, that there was more danger of their getting down after they got to the transfer and getting tramped to death than before. Then he said lots of stockmen who tried to get to town from the transfer in the night and had got killed, and some got their legs cut off by trains that were all the time switching on the transfer tracks. He said if the Humane Society took half the pains to protect the shippers that they did the stock being shipped he thought it would be

better. He said a shipper was a human being even if
he did look like a orangoutang just dragged out of a
Chicago sewer when he got through to Omaha with a
shipment of livestock. I thought maybe he was getting personal, so told him he didn't look so fine himself; that I thought anyone who resembled a jackass
in a Wyoming blizzard hadn't any call to make reflect-
tions on other people's looks. Just then the switch
engine coupled onto his train and hauled him and his
stock off to the unloading chutes, and I was kinda glad
he was gone, as I had conceived a dislike to him anyway. I can't bear anyone who makes disagreeable reflections and comparisons on one's personal appearance when one isn't looking their best, especially a
person who ain't got anything to brag of themselves.

THE FARMER'S PRAYER.

I looked on the other side of me and saw another
stock train with a group of four or five stockmen on
top the cars. They were huddled down together in the
snow and wet, and I thought at first one of them was
making a speech, but soon discovered he was praying.
It turned out one of their number was dying from ill
health and the exposure of the night before, they hav-

ing been there all night waiting for the switch engine
to haul them to the chutes.   They were a bunch of Nebraska farmers who had bought some feeders in Omaha sometime previous, shipped them out to their farms
a couple hundred miles west, fed up their corn crop
and was bringing the cattle back.   The man that wa
praying seemed to be a son and partner of the dying
man, and was telling the Lord the whole transaction
from a to izard.   Whether he was doing this to relieve
his own feelings, or whether he thought the Lord
would size his father up as an honest man in place of
a sucker, it's hard to tell.   Anyway, you could tell by
his prayer that him and his dying father had got the
worst of the deal all the way through.   What I heard
of his prayer run something like this:

"O Lord, Thou knowest how Thy humble servants have been the victims of designing and unscru-
pulous men.   Thou knowest, Lord, how a hooked-nosed
Sheeny first induced Thy poor servants to buy of him
a lot of crooked-backed, narrow-hipped, long-tailed,
high-on-the-rump, ewe-necked, dehorned, Southern
steers, and how they had kept them off of water for
seven days, waiting for a sale, and then let them drink
till their stomachs was like unto bass drums, when

they weighed them up to Thy deceived servants, and then, O Lord, Thy wretched servants, not having any money to pay for them, we had to go to a grasping commission man and, O Lord, Thou knowest how he did charge us usury cent for cent and all kinds of percent, how he figured up interest on the cost of the steers, then figured interest on that interest, then figured interest on the interest that he had figured on the interest, then figured a commission for buying them, then another commission for selling them, then figured the interest on the commission, then figured the interest on the interest that he had figured on the commission; and, how when we had got these steers home, two of them were dead, three were cripples, five were lump-jaws, and how their feet were so large, and they had such wise, old-fashioned countenances, we were behooved to look into their mouths to determine by their teeth how old they were, and Thy astonished servants discovered that in place of two year-olds, as was represented, they were a great many times two years old; and how many times when we had a little fat on their ribs, they saw someone afoot, and becoming frightened, ran round and round the feed lots till they were poorer than ever, and some there was that escaping over the fence were never seen by Thy servants any more, they having disappeared · over the hills and in adjacent corn fields; and Thou knowest how we were always sober, law-abiding citizens till we were inveigled into buying these imitation steers, and since that time have lived in a constant round of excitement, terror and riot."

The switch engine now coupled on to the dying man's stock train and pulled it away to the chutes, so I didn't hear the last of the prayer. Probably his commission man heard it after he got through explaining why the steers didn't bring any more money.

CHAPTER XXIV.

THE FINAL ROUNDUP.

Two railroad men of mighty brain,
The steadfast friends of true cowmen;
No matter which the first you name,
We all love George Crosby and Charlie Lane.

And if in this story, they should see
Some mentioned evil, for which a remedy
That's in their power and can be used,
They'll fix it so the shipper is less abused.

Of all things needed, and it's a crying shame,
Is some kind of toilet room on each stock train;
In regard to fires, let the shippers agree,
Whether they'll be froze or roasted into eternity.

Have a call-boy escort with lantern bright,
When at division stations we come in darkest night;
To save our anxiety, fear and doubt,
Put us on the right way-car that's going out.

To the stockyards company a suggestion could be made,
If they expect to keep and gain more trade;
When our cattle are delivered on their transfer track,
Try and unload them, or else we'll ship them back.

If one or two of these evils should be wiped away
By these suggestions in this humble lay,
Then will I rejoice and forget the days of toil
When I composed this work and burnt the midnight oil.

14—

The Denver Union Stock Yard Co., Denver, Colo.

Greatest Stocker, Feeder and Fat Stock Market in the West:

♪ ♪ Capacity—15,000 Cattle; 10,000 Hogs; 30,000 Sheep; 5,000 Horses. ♪ ♪

G. W. BALLENTINE, V.-Pres. and Gen. Mgr.   J. W. HURD, Asst. Treasurer.   H. PETRIE, Superintendent,

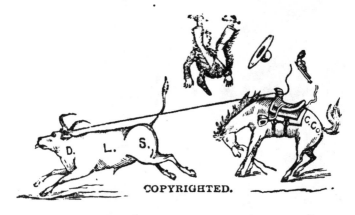

CPSIA information can be obtained
at www.ICGtesting.com
Printed in the USA
BVHW091354020119
536867BV00019B/368/P